MIDNIGHT SERENADE

A Fantasy Novel

FETRICIA ZENYOKA

Djs legacy incorporated

MIDNIGHT SERENADE

At 32 years young, Zenyoka, proudly resides in Florida, holding onto her South Carolina native roots with pride. As a devoted single mother to two remarkable boys, she finds solace and strength in her unshakeable faith, believing wholeheartedly that with God's guidance, all things are possible. Zenyoka has navigated through life's challenges with courage and resilience, triumphing over the shadows of domestic violence and her mental health battles. Discovering solace and healing through the power of writing, she found a safe haven in self-expression during her darkest moments. Guided by her personal mantra #doingtriciS***, which means "Living unapologetically in the rawest form of self, without pause." She embodies the essence of living authentically and unapologetically, celebrating her true self and inspiring others to do the same. With a profound passion for championing women's empowerment, Zenyoka finds joy in witnessing women break free from societal constraints and embrace their unique identities. Her heart beats for empowering women to rewrite their own narratives, conquer their fears, and become the architects of their destinies. Despite facing moments of self-doubt and numerous starts and stops over the past eight years, Zenyoka has persevered in her journey to bring her dreams to life. Through her extraordinary gift for storytelling, she transforms dreams into tangible realities, crafting narratives and characters that will capture you from the first chapter. Her upcoming fiction book delves into the complexities of a woman's journey as she unravels the dark secrets of her mother's past, torn between seeking justice and embracing love. Through her captivating storytelling, Zenyoka invites readers to take a journey with her, because every story will be a journey. The release of her first book serves as a reminder to her, and to everyone else that circumstances should never hinder one's pursuit of their dreams. She encourages women to live authentically, to follow their hearts, and to make choices that resonate with their true selves. In the end, Zenyoka urges women to take charge of their destinies, to live for themselves, and to pursue their passions with determination and purpose. It doesn't matter when you do it, as long as you do it!

Mom

You are my rock, my guiding light, and my biggest supporter. When I hit rock bottom, you were there to lift me up. Whenever I call, you come running to my side. You have my back through everything in life, in all things. You are the reason I stand as the woman I am today. Your love, strength, and unmatched belief in me have made all things possible. This book is as much yours as it is mine, for without you, none of this would have been achievable. I dedicate these words to you, with all my heart and gratitude.

Pudd

You are my ride or die, my partner in crime, and my person, all rolled into one. Thank you for always having my back, even when I doubted myself. Your faith in me has been unmatched, pushing me to chase my biggest dreams. Always pushing me to reach for the stars. Through all the crazy adventures and tough times, you've been my rock and my source of endless laughter. This book is a tribute to our lifelong friendship and the bond that keeps us together. I dedicate these words to you, with all my love and appreciation.

CONTENTS

First Printing, 2024

Prologue

The hospital waiting room, an endless corridor of anxiety, held Amara captive in the haunting echoes of uncertainty. The familiar chair beneath her seemed to offer little comfort, its worn fabric bearing witness to the shared stories of countless lives, but tonight, it cradled her in a solitude she had never known. Amara's thoughts retraced the steps that led her here, back to the jarring call that had disrupted the rhythm of her day. A voice on the other end had urged her to rush to the hospital, an urgent plea that sent her heart into a panicked frenzy. As she moved through the sterile corridors of the hospital, the memory of that call lingered like a persistent shadow, amplifying the anxiety that tightened her chest. The door creaked open, and a Doctor entered the waiting area. His eyes scanned the room, searching for a saddened spouse, as he knew the news he was coming out to provide saddened news as it related to someone's husband." Their gazes locked, and a heavy silence filled the air as he approached, carrying news that would redefine Amara's world. "Amara Bishop" Dr. Reynolds' voice carried a weight that mirrored the gravity of the news he was about to share. "Yeah, that's me. Are you my Husbands doctor? Is he ok? What's going on with Adrian? Where's my husband?" Amara's voice quivered, her eyes pleading for reassurance. "I'm Dr. Reynolds. I've got some tough news about your husband, Adrian." The weight of his words hung in the air, the room tilting on its axis. Panic surged through Amara, a knot tightening in her stomach. "There was a car accident. I'm sorry to tell you this, but Adrian didn't make it." The room seemed to close in as Dr. Reynolds uttered those fateful words, "There was a car accident.

I'm sorry to tell you this, but Adrian didn't make it." The air itself became heavier, hit with an unbearable truth that Amara couldn't fathom. Time stopped. It hung suspended in the reality of those words, and Amara struggled to process the unthinkable. The world around her unraveled like a nightmare she couldn't wake up from, and she clung to the edges of her seat as if trying to anchor herself in the chaos. "No... no, that can't be right," she murmured, the words escaping her lips in a desperate whisper, as if hoping to deny the horror of the news. But reality, merciless and unforgiving, pressed on. Dr. Reynolds hesitated; his eyes filled with an empathy that only deepened the tragedy. "I wish I could give you more details, but the accident was severe, his car caught fire and was engulfed in flames. His entire body... it was badly burned, almost unrecognizable. Dr. Reynolds pulled out a ring from his pocket, it was Adrian's wedding ring. Dr. Reynolds knew his spouse would want to confirm that it was her husband lying back there, lifeless." Amara's hands trembled uncontrollably, one hand holding his ring, and her fingers grasping the edges of the chair for support. The room tilted as despair and disbelief collided within her, threatening to consume every ounce of strength. Suddenly, the ground beneath her seemed to shift, and without warning, she crumpled. A sharp cry tore from her throat, echoing the raw pain that surged through her. The hospital staff, trained to handle such heart-wrenching moments, moved swiftly to her side, attempting to provide solace and support. In her desperate attempt to escape the unyielding reality, Amara fought against the restraining hands of the nursing staff. "Adrian! Adrian!" she screamed, the intensity of her anguish echoing through the sterile halls. Her voice cracked with the weight of grief, a haunting melody that echoed the depths of her despair. "Mrs. Bishop, please, please," the nurses pleaded, their voices filled with compassion but also the obvious recognition of the harsh reality they were trying to shield her from. The struggle between Amara and the nurses intensified as she fought to break free, her cries for her husband becoming more desperate with each passing moment. “No, let me go! I need to see him! Adrian!” Amara's voice wavered between a loud scream and a broken plea; the pain of her loss etched into every syllable. The hospital staff, overwhelmed by the intense display of grief, held firm, their attempts to console Amara punctuated by her anguished cries. In the midst of the confusion, Amara's world crumbled, and the sterile hospital walls became a witness to the unraveling of a love abruptly silenced. The echoes of her screams lingered; a haunting reminder of a heartache that seemed overwhelming. Numbly, she paused standing looking at the staff with deep eyes of sorrow. The world reduced to a blur of pain and grief. Dr. Reynolds and the staff offered their condolences before retreating, leaving her alone in the oppressive silence. Leaving the hospital, Amara felt the weight of the world pressing down on her shoulders. The journey home was a blur, the windshield wipers doing little to clear the storm on her window or the one brewing within her. She arrived at the doorstep of a house that had once been a sanctuary, now echoing with the haunting absence of Adrian. Entering the silent home, the emptiness swallowed her. She moved through the rooms, each step a painful reminder of the void Adrian's absence left behind. Glancing at the pictures that adorned the walls, she lingered, tears tracing the contours of cherished memories. The hallway, once a path brightened by the promise of a shared future, now stretched before her like an uncharted territory of grief. Amara moved through it slowly, her fingertips grazing the memories etched in the walls. The weight of solitude pressed against her, and the tears that had been held at bay began to flow. Amara walked into the bedroom with slow steps, her eyes scanning the bed. It hit her that Adrian wouldn't sleep on his usual side tonight, and the room felt empty, a lonely reminder of what used to be. The air in the room felt heavy, filled with the loneliness that now hung in the air. She found herself in the bathroom lost, staring at herself in the mirror. Her eyes reflected a deep sadness, a heavy feeling in her chest that made breathing difficult. After a moment, her phone's ringer broke the silence, reminding her of a life that had changed. She powered her phone off, she just wanted to be alone. Entering the closet, she was surrounded by the smell of Adrian's cologne. It was like a comforting hug from many memories, making her way through his clothes, touching them, inhaling the scent that still lingered. The closet became a safe space, a haven where it still felt like a piece of him was there. Each breath she took was a reminder of their shared life, a moment to be with the memories that clung to the fabric. In this simple act, Amara tried to find solace in the midst of overwhelming grief. She grabbed one of Adrian's sweaters, holding it close, she sank onto the floor, the floodgates of grief opening. As she lay there, the sweater cradled against her, Amara's mind drifted to the happy memories she and Adrian had shared. The laughter, the shared dreams, the quiet moments that had built the foundation of their love. Tears blurred the line between past and present, and she cried herself to sleep, the weight of loss and the weight of the sweater wrapped in the silent darkness. When morning arrived, it carried with it the harsh reality of a world forever changed. Amara was roused from her fitful sleep by the insistent chime of the doorbell. Disoriented and heavy with grief, she stumbled to the front door. On the opposite side, Harrison stood, his gaze echoing a shared sorrow. Amara looked exhausted, her eyes red and swollen from endless tears. She was not prepared for what she was about to hear, for the truth, would shatter her world. And there, standing on her doorstep, was Harrison, his face etched with a mix of sadness and determination. "Harrison, what do you want?" she asked, her voice filled with a mix of anger and pain. Harrison took a deep breath, his voice heavy with the truth he was about to drop. "Amara, we need to talk. I know you probably don't wanna hear shit right now, but this is important, and it can't wait." Amara reluctantly eased the door open and let Harrison in. He followed her to the kitchen, where she was brewing some coffee. Harrison knew he had to tell her the truth, even though it would tear her apart. "Look, I know today might not be the best time, but what I have to tell you is something you need to know." Harrison looked down and took a deep breath, Amara had just lost her husband, he knew the news he was about to share was going to break Amara down even more. "Adrian, he wasn't just some regular dude. He wasn't just into real-estate and construction, even though he had that shit going too." Amar's irritation grew, her patience wearing thin. "Harrison, get to the point. What is so important?" Harrison took a deep breath, bracing himself for the storm that was about to hit. "Amara, Adrian was a drug dealer. And I ain't talking about no small-time shit. He was the boss, the Heffe, the top dog in the game. He was the one you had to go through to make some real fucking money." Amar's eyes widened in shock and disbelief. "No, no, my husband wasn't a drug dealer. He owned properties, and we managed that shit together. We got checks in the mail every month, all legit." Harrison looked down, then back at Amara, his voice filled with a mix of guilt and sorrow. "I know this shit sounds crazy, but I've been right there with him for the past five years. I watched him go from hustling dime bags, managing street corners, to building a fucking empire. Yeah, he owned properties, but those tenants were his people, his crew and their families. Anger and confusion swirled within her, threatening to consume her. "So, you're telling me my husband, my gentle, kind, sweet, loving husband was some kind of criminal? He was what some kind of monster on the streets? No, hell no Harrison what the fuck is going on? You telling me he kept all this shit from me? He put my life in danger every fucking day, and I knew nothing about it?" Harrison's voice softened; his tone filled with regret. "Nah, Amara, he didn't want to put you at risk. He wanted to protect you, keep you away from the darkness. He figured the less you knew, the better. But sometimes, the choices we make have consequences we don't see coming. But he was getting out. After he met you that's all he could talk about getting out and living right. Yesterday was our last deal but I guess somebody didn't want us out." Amara's voice trembled with a mix of sadness and anger. "What does that mean?" Harrison took a deep breath, his voice filled with a mix of pain and resolution. "Adrian's car accident wasn't no accident. He was killed." Amara gasped; her eyes widened as she grabbed her chest at this news. "Someone ambushed him when he was coming out of the warehouse. There was a crash and then I saw this man in all black go in his trunk and take a suitcase. It had 7.5 million in it Amara." Amara began to hyperventilate, her world crumbling around her. She thought she knew the man she laid down next to every night, but now she didn't know what to believe. She couldn't believe that Adrian could be capable of things Harrison was saying. Memories flashed in her mind, the long nights he spent working, the mysterious phone calls all times of the night, the sudden weekend trips, his ability to rent out entire restaurants, just for the two of them, it all started to make sense. But Harrison wasn't done yet. He had one more bomb to drop, one more truth that he knew would push Amara to the edge. "Amara looked off into space, her eyes filled with pain and sorrow. She had no words, to express the betrayal she felt. Harrison knew he had to convince her to get out of town. He still didn't know who killed Adrian or why exactly. But he knew the lifestyle they had lived they had did a lot to people over time. He knew everyone was aware he had gotten married and didn't want Amara caught in the crossfire. He had promised Adrian he would always protect Amara, and the only way to protect her now was for her to go away. "Listen, Amara, Adrian left me a key to a safe deposit box. He told me if anything ever happened to him, for me to give you this key. Everything you need to know, everything you need is in this box. Grab your passport, get what's inside, and disappear. Find some small ass city out, stay under the radar and run. Harrison handed her a phone, "Keep this phone with you. When it's safe I'll call you ok. Someone killed my best friend, and we not stopping until we find out who." Adrian grabbed Amara's hand, "There's a war coming, Amara, and you gotta be gone." Harrison hugged Amara as he turned to walk out.

CHAPTER 1

Love on Aisle 3

Amara gracefully navigated the aisles of the upscale grocery store, her hazel-brown eyes scanning the shelves for the items on her list. The ambient hum of the store surrounded her, and she moved through the bustling aisles with a presence that commanded attention. Her sister locs, naturally beautiful and cascading down her shoulders, added an air of effortless elegance to her appearance. Dressed in a stylish yet comfortable ensemble, she exuded confidence that caught the eyes of those around her. On the other side of the store, Adrian, a tall and handsome black man with rich brown skin, browsed the produce section. His attire, a meticulously chosen sweat suit that showcased his well-defined physique, spoke of both comfort and style. Adrian's waves were perfectly cut, adding an extra layer of refinement to his appearance. As he reached for a piece of fruit, his eyes shifted, and his gaze locked onto Amara. Their eyes met, and a magnetic connection sparked between them. Time seemed to pause as Adrian couldn't tear his eyes away from Amara's captivating presence. Something about her drew him in, an allure that went beyond physical attraction. Amara, feeling his gaze upon her, glanced back, and their eyes held for a lingering moment before a playful smile curved on her lips. Unable to resist the pull, Adrian approached her with a flirtatious energy. "Excuse me," he said, his voice smooth and confident. "I couldn't help but notice you from across the aisle. I was wondering if I could join you on your shopping adventure," Adrian said, a playful smile tugging at the corners of his lips. Amara chuckled, a warm twinkle in her eyes. "Well, aren't you the adventurous type, approaching strangers in the grocery store? What's your angle here? Are you a shopping expert or just in need of a snack buddy?" Adrian grinned, playing along. "A bit of both, actually. I figure grocery shopping is a social event waiting to happen. I'm more of a health nut, and I see your cart is full of all the best snacks. I could use some expert advice. You up for the challenge?" Amara raised an eyebrow, full of skepticism. "Expert advice, huh? You might be biting off more than you can chew. I'm a foodie, believe it or not. But sure, why not? Consider yourself my official snack apprentice for today". Adrian smiled, extending his hand. "By the way, I'm Adrian. Nice to meet you." Amara shook his hand, her eyes sparkling. "Amara. Pleasure to meet you too, Adrian." Adrian's curiosity piqued. "So, Amara, where are you from?" “Atlanta actually, what about you?” Adrian smiled “Same, Atlanta is home for me.” Amara's eyes widened in surprise. “You know, Atlanta has grown so much, I hardly meet people who are actually from here. It's always nice to meet someone from back home." Adrian chuckled, a sense of familiarity settling between them. "I couldn't agree more. Atlanta has a certain charm that's hard to find anywhere else. What part of the city did you grow up in?" Amara smiled, a nostalgic glimmer in her eyes. "Oh, I was born and raised in Decatur. What about you?” “I actually grew up in East Atlanta. I always loved living here in the city, I don’t think I really would ever want to leave.” As they continued strolling through the store, their conversation delved into more deeper topics. “So, Amara what do you do? If you don’t mind me asking.” Amara’s eyes lit up she loved to talk about her work. “I’m a photographer actually.” Adrian was surprised, he wouldn’t have thought she was photographer, but he wanted to hear more. “Why photography?” Amara's eyes lit up as she spoke passionately about her photography. "You know, there's something magical about freezing a moment in time. It's like I can capture the emotions, the essence of a moment, and preserve it forever. Sometimes, a photograph can convey more than words ever could." Adrian nodded, a genuine curiosity in his eyes. "That's incredible. I've always admired people who have the ability to see the world through a different lens, to capture the beauty in the simplest of things. It takes a special kind of talent." Amara smiled, appreciating his understanding. "Thank you, It's not just about taking pretty pictures for me; it's about telling stories, evoking emotions, and making people feel something when they look at my work. It's a way for me to connect with others on a deeper level." Adrian leaned in, his voice filled with admiration. "I can see the passion in your eyes when you talk about it. It's inspiring. Do you have a favorite subject or style of photography?" Amara's face lit up, eager to share. "I love capturing candid moments, the raw and unposed shots that reveal the true essence of a person or a situation. Street photography is a personal favorite of mine. There's something so captivating about the energy of the streets, the stories unfolding in every corner." Adrian nodded, a smile playing on his lips. "That's fascinating. I can only imagine how powerful those images must be. I understand why you love doing it, but what made you interested in it, in the first place?" Amara's smile softened, a hint of nostalgia in her eyes. She took a moment to gather her thoughts before speaking. "Well, growing up my mother she was amazing. She was so beautiful inside and out; and I was her entire world. Her and my dad they weren’t together, but they were literally best friends. She was the heart and soul of our family, and one thing she always was doing, was capturing precious moments with her camera. Every family gathering, every holiday, she would be there, documenting our lives in a photo. Some of my family hated it, but she could have cared less. I mean she didn't even care how you looked; she would take your picture regardless." Her voice quivered as she recounted a specific memory, her 13th birthday. "I remember it was my 13th birthday and she had picked me out this beautiful white dress to wear, she did my hair, and it was the best day in the world to me, I was officially a teenager. She had bought so many disposable cameras I knew she was going to be taking pictures the entire day. It was time to cut my cake, and I begged her to let me do it. Somehow, I slipped, tripped over my shoe, and fell face first in my cake. I was so embarrassed and wanted to cry. But my mother being her, with all of her make up on, and her hair freshly done, she smashed her face into the cake. We looked at each other and completely fell out in laughter, my dad had picked up her camera and captured those priceless moments of just pure raw joy and laughter." Her voice wavered slightly, a mix of sadness and warmth. "Amara's voice trembled, tears streaming down her face. "But the next morning... everything changed. I woke up, expecting to hear my mother's voice, making breakfast, and getting ready for church. But she wasn't there. I went downstairs, searching for her, and when I entered her room, my heart shattered. There she was, lying on her bed, quiet, motionless. My mother had taken her own life." The weight of the loss hung heavy in the air as Amara continued, her voice filled with a mixture of sorrow and warmth. "There was a note by her bed, addressed to me. It contained so many words, so many emotions. But the one thing that has stayed with me, the one thing that echoes in my heart every day, was her message to 'live in the rawest form of yourself, unapologetically without pause.'" Amara took a deep breath, her voice quivering with the weight of her grief. "Losing her was the hardest thing I've ever experienced. I had so many unanswered questions, so much pain to work through. But in the midst of my grief, I found solace in going through her old photo albums. Each image was like a time capsule, preserving the memories and emotions of our family's journey. It was through those photographs that I realized they were more than just pictures. They were a living legacy, a way for us to hold onto the love and joy we shared. And in that moment, I knew I wanted to carry on my mother's legacy, to capture the beauty of life and create lasting memories for others." Amara's eyes met Adrian's, and she could see the genuine empathy reflected in his gaze. She felt a sense of comfort and understanding wash over her as he reached out to gently wipe away her tear. His touch was gentle, his presence reassuring. Adrian's voice was soft and filled with heartfelt compassion as he spoke. "Amara," he whispered, his words carrying the weight of his empathy. "I can't even begin to imagine the depth of your pain and the profound loss you've experienced. Your mother sounds like an extraordinary woman, and it's evident that her love and spirit continue to live on through you." He paused, his eyes locked with hers, wanting to convey his understanding and support. "You turned your pain into purpose and that's very hard for some people to do. But you did that, I know your mother is proud of you." Amara took a deep breath, her eyes reflecting a mixture of gratitude and a desire to shift the conversation. She smiled softly at Adrian, a glimmer of curiosity in her gaze. "Enough about me, I can be a talker if you haven't noticed." she said, her voice filled with warmth. "I've shared a lot about myself, so now I want to know more about you, Adrian. What do you do?" Adrian returned her smile, his eyes lighting up with enthusiasm. "Well, actually I'm in real estate. I've been doing real estate probably about 10 years now. It's a rewarding profession, being able to help others find their perfect place to call home." Amara's eyes sparkled with interest. "That's dope. I've always admired people who have an eye for design and the ability to create beautiful spaces. I bet it feels so rewarding helping people become homeowners." Adrian nodded, his enthusiasm evident. "Absolutely!

There's something special about witnessing the excitement and happiness on someone's face when they find their dream home. It's a privilege to be a part of that journey." As they continued to stroll through the store, Amara's eyes widened as she checked the time on her phone. She let out a soft gasp, a mix of surprise and regret washing over her face. "Oh, my goodness, Adrian! I just realized I'm running late for a lunch. I can't believe we've been wandering around this store for over an hour. Time really flew by with such great company," she said, a hint of disappointment in her voice. Adrian's smile softened, understanding her predicament. "I completely lost track of time too, Amara. It's been such a pleasure getting to know you. I'm sorry if I interrupted your shopping plans." Amara waved off his apology, a playful glint in her eyes. "Oh, don't worry about it, Adrian. I didn't even get what I came into the store for, but it's okay. The company was well worth it." As they made their way towards the exit, Adrian walked her to her car, a smooth confidence emanating from him. Adrian leaned casually against Amara's car, his magnetic presence captivating her. His voice dripped with a playful charm as he spoke, his words flowing effortlessly. "Amara," he said, his voice smooth as silk, "I must admit, I simply couldn't let you leave without finding a way to stay in touch. Would it be too forward of me to ask for your number? I'd love nothing more than to continue our captivating conversation." Amara's heart skipped a beat as she felt the rush of excitement coursing through her veins. A smile tugged at the corners of her lips, unable to resist the charm that radiated from Adrian. A soft giggle escaped her lips as she replied, her voice filled with a hint of playfulness. "Forward? Not at all. In fact, I would have been offended if you didn't ask. As they swiftly exchanged contact information, their fingers briefly brushing against each other's phones, a spark of anticipation filled the air. There was an undeniable chemistry between them, a connection that seemed to transcend the boundaries of a chance encounter. Amara couldn't help but be captivated by Adrian's smooth demeanor and his way with words. It was as if he had a natural talent for making her feel special, leaving her yearning for more. Amara couldn't help but feel a sense of excitement and curiosity about what the future might hold. She knew she had only met Adrian an hour ago, but something felt different. She couldn't put her finger on it, but the promise of continuing their conversation, of exploring this newfound connection, filled her with a thrilling anticipation. And as they bid each other farewell, their smiles lingering, they both knew that this encounter had the potential to be the beginning of something remarkable. In that moment, they couldn't help but feel a shared excitement, a sense of possibility that danced in their hearts. As Amara drove away, her mind filled with thoughts of Adrian, she couldn't help but smile. She was late for her lunch, but she decided she wasn't going to mention the encounter to her best friend Sasha. She knew Sasha would get excited and with her luck in dating there was a chance this Adrian guy wouldn't be around anyway. The jingle of the cafe's door announced Amara's arrival, and Sasha's face lit up as her best friend approached their favorite corner table. They shared a hug that spoke volumes about the years of friendship they held dear. “Sasha, my favorite person in the entire world!” Amara grinned, her eyes sparkling with genuine joy. Sasha chuckled, “I better be your favorite! Otherwise, we was gone have a problem.” As they settled into their seats, the atmosphere buzzed with the familiarity of shared stories and inside jokes. The clinking of cups and distant chatter provided the perfect backdrop to their catch-up session. Amara, however, seemed a tad preoccupied, her eyes randomly darting to her phone. Sasha couldn't help but notice the subtle smiles that played on Amara's lips which raised her curiosity. “Why you got that look on your face? And why you keep looking at your phone? What you got going on?” Sasha nudged her playfully. Amara's cheeks flushed, and she looked up with a mischievous glint in her eyes. “I was just making sure I wasn’t missing any calls. You know sometimes the signal is bad in here.” Sasha raised an eyebrow, a knowing smirk forming. “Umm, You sure that’s it? I mean because you are staring at that phone, with that big ass goofy smile on your face. Something I need to know?” Amara chuckled, “No, it’s nothing to mention right now, trust me, but when there is something to tell you'll be the first to know.” “Okk, alright fine,” their laughter echoed in the cozy cafe, blending seamlessly with the hum of the coffee machines. The friends exchanged tales of work, life, and the local community gossip. As Sasha took a sip of her coffee, she couldn't help but notice Amara's subtle smiles and the way her eyes sparkled. Sasha and Amara had been friends since 5th grade, over 20 years, she knew something was up. Sasha leaned in, her eyes wide with curiosity. “Amara, spill it! You've been grinning at that damn phone, like you waiting on somebody to call it. What's going on?” Amara's laughter bubbled up, and she took a moment, her eyes reflecting a mixture of excitement and uncertainty. “Ok fine, but don’t get excited just listen Sash. Remember I told you I needed to go to the store and restock up on my snacks, and drinks right.” Sasha engaged in the story “Yea, so what you enter a lottery for free food or something, like why you staring at that phone?” Amara laughing at her response, “Listen, so I was at the store I met this guy, Adrian. But when I say guy, I don’t mean just a “guy” I met a man. A tall 6ft, dark skin, beautiful smile, smelling like he just stepped off the front of an Essence magazine. Sash, this man was beautiful, shoot he’s the reason I was late getting here. We walked around the store talking for over an hour, hell I forgot to even get my damn groceries.” Amara closed her eyes remembering the encounter and how it made her feel. “I mean you know how you watch a movie, and you see two people meet each other, and it seems like love at first sight. You normally think to yourself this shit don’t happen in real life. Sasha! It happened. I mean I won’t say love at first sight, but I will say it was a connection I have never felt in my life. I don't know, it was something about him, I can't get him out of my head since we met." Sasha gave her a excited look, "Oh, shit, girl, you sitting over there with this kind of tea talking about you when there's something to tell I'll be the first to know, well Bitch this is something to tell. Spill it." Amara laughed and took a deep breath, her mind flashing back to the aisles of the store where their paths had crossed. "Sasha, he's got this smile that captivates you, and his eyes it was like they twinkled. I couldn't stop staring into them, it was like I got lost in them. They were brown and warm, kind of felt like he could see right into my soul. When he walked up to me in the store, shit I smelled him before he got to me. His cologne drew me in like a trance. Shit, had me watering at the mouth. There was just something about the way he looked at me. Like I was the only person in the entire store. Being in his presence was comforting and familiar. It felt like I had known him my entire life. And his style! You could look at him and tell it was effortless. It was just a simple sweat suit, but he wore it like it was tailor-made just for him. He was just so peaceful." Sasha's playful grin widened. "OMG, Amara!" Amara's cheeks flushed, and she grinned back. "Oh, and he funny as hell. Girl he had me laughing all up and through Trader Joes you hear me. It felt so easy, so natural. It's been so long since someone had that effect on me, you know?" Sasha's eyes softened, "Damnnnn, girl." Amara nodded; her gaze distant as if lost in the memory of her earlier encounter. "It's just a feeling, Sash. But I haven't been able to shake it, since the moment he asked my name. I can't even describe the feeling, because I feel silly. I mean I met him in the grocery store literally just a few hours ago. I shouldn't be feeling like this right? I don't know, maybe it's nothing, or maybe... maybe it's something." Sasha grinned, her eyes reflecting the shared history and countless conversations they'd had about love and life. Sasha knew her friend had, had a hard time when it came to finding love. She knew her friend was a great person;

Amara was beautiful and successful. She knew her friend deserved something real for a change. “Well, my friend, if anybody deserves happiness it is you. Amara you are one of the most beautiful humans I know, inside and out. You have this huge heart that would give anything you could to help a stranger. And let’s be real you really could be outside having your way and popping shit, but you chose to remain down to earth and humble. You are “IT” girl and nobody who meets you can deny that. Any man on this earth would be lucky to even occupy the same space as you.” Amara was so grateful for her Sasha. One thing Sasha never let her forget is how great she was, even during the times she didn’t really feel all that great about herself. “Sasha, I love you girl, I don’t know how I could have ever done life without.” Sasha smiled “You would be exactly where needed to be with or without me sis. You’re, you, and that alone is powerful enough to shake up any room. Now, when Mr. Perfect calls and you finish all that smooth talking, make sure I’m the next call as soon as yall hang up. I want all the tea fresh off the stove baby. Amara chuckled, a mixture of excitement and nervousness lingering in her expression. She knew that Sasha was always there to support her, to celebrate her victories and lend a listening ear during the uncertainties of love. As they sat down at the table, ready to indulge in their lunch, Amara couldn't help but feel a renewed sense of hope. The encounter with Adrian had sparked something within her, a flicker of excitement for what the future might hold. In that moment, surround by the warmth of her friendship and the possibilities of something new and exciting, Amara felt a surge of anticipation. This was just the beginning, and she was ready to embrace whatever lied ahead. Amara found herself back at home, her mind swirling with thoughts and emotions. The guy from the store had left a lasting impression, a spark that ignited in her heart. She couldn't help but wonder why she hadn't heard from him yet. The connection they shared felt real, and she couldn't shake off the anticipation of his call.

"Maybe I should just text him," she mused out loud, twirling her phone in her hand. She debated whether it would be too forward to make the first move. Just as she was lost in her thoughts, her phone's ringtone startled her, causing her to drop it to the floor. She hurriedly picked it up, hoping she hadn't missed an important call. Seeing the name "Adrian" on the screen made her heart skip a beat, and her stomach did a little flip. With a mix of excitement and nerves, Amara answered the call, her voice filled with a hint of anticipation. "Hello," she greeted, her voice slightly higher than usual, betraying her nervousness. "Hey, beautiful," Adrian's smooth voice flowed through the phone, instantly easing any tension. "I'm sorry for taking so long to reach out. Work got a bit crazy, but I'm glad I finally got the chance to call. How was the rest of your day?" Amara couldn't help but smile, her voice filled with warmth. "It was good. I met up with my best friend for lunch, caught up with her, and then had to go back to the grocery store to pick up the things I forgot," she chuckled. "After that, I've just been at home working. Overall, it's been a pretty great day. How about you? How was the rest of your day?" Adrian's voice carried a sense of excitement as he shared his day with Amara. "The rest of my day was filled with driving around, showing properties to clients. I always try to make their experience exceptional. But I have to admit, you were on my mind the entire time. And now, talking to you, it feels like the perfect way to end an amazing day." A brief moment of silence hung in the air, their unspoken connection weaving through the phone lines. It was as if their smiles were mirroring each other, creating a special bond. Adrian knew that being in Amara's presence, even in silence, was enough for him. Breaking the silence, Adrian gently prompted, "Tell me about your best friend, the one you met for lunch. What's the story there, how did you guys become best friends?" Amara felt a sense of relief as Adrian broke the silence, allowing her to share more about her closest friend. She took a deep breath, her voice filled with fondness and nostalgia. "Sasha, my best friend, honestly she is more like family to me. We actually met back in fourth grade when she transferred to our school. She always seemed so quiet and sad, and no one really paid much attention to her. One day, I just sat with her at lunch, we didn't say a word to each other. It went on for about two weeks, I sat with her we ate lunch, then we went to class. One day we were sitting there in silence, eating our food. Then, out of nowhere, she turned to me and said, 'My mom died.' It was such a raw and honest moment," Amara explained, her voice reflecting the depth of their connection. "After that, we became inseparable. Sasha spent a lot of time at my house because my mom struggled with severe depression. You know at a younger age, you don't fully understand it, but having Sasha around brought a sense of peace during those difficult times. We supported each other through thick and thin," Amara continued, her voice tinged with gratitude. She paused for a moment; her voice filled with emotion as she shared a pivotal moment. "When I found my mother dead the day after my birthday, Sasha was the first person I called. Not an ambulance, not my dad, not the police, but Sasha. She rushed over to my house and found me completely broken. Without saying a word, she called 911 and stayed by my side. Sasha became my rock during that time. She slept on the floor next to me for the next couple of nights, just there to give support when I needed it the most." Amara's voice trembled as she recounted the painful memory to Adrian. "On the day of my mother's funeral, I felt completely numb. I hadn't shed a tear, spoken a word, or even slept since I found her lifeless body. It was as if I were stuck in a never-ending nightmare. Standing there, gazing at my mother's casket being lowered into the ground, I felt empty, so broken." Adrian listened attentively, his heart breaking for Amara. He could sense the weight of her grief, the heaviness of her loss. "I can't even begin to imagine how difficult that must have been for you," he said softly. Amara took a deep breath; she could hear her voice quivering. "And then, out of nowhere, Sasha appeared by my side. She was holding two brown paper bags in her hands, with a packed lunch. We sat down right in front of my mother's grave, opened the bags, it was the exact lunch we both had the first time we spoke to each other back in the 4th grade. I was about to take a bite of my sandwich, I looked at Sasha and whispered, 'My mom died.' "In that instant, all the pain, the sorrow, the pent-up emotions, they all came pouring out. I cried like I had never cried before. It hadn't hit me really that my mother was gone forever until right then. Sasha sat there with me for two more hours, holding me, crying with me, and reminding me that I wasn't alone." Adrian's voice was filled with empathy as he responded, "Amara, I am so sorry, you had to experience a pain of that magnitude. And Sasha, sounds like an incredible friend, you are lucky to have her in your life. Amara nodded; her voice filled with gratitude. "Yes, Sasha has been my rock. She's more than just a best friend; she's my person." Adrian's voice softened with understanding. "I can see why she means so much to you. Having someone like Sasha by your side, someone who understands your pain and stands with you through it all, is a true blessing. Not that many people get to experience a friendship like that in their lifetime. "I hope, if you're okay with it, I can meet her one day," Adrian expressed, hinting at his intention to stick around. Amara's excitement grew, and she couldn't help but smile. "Well, of course! Trust me, she's anxious to meet you too. I mean, if you're around, not saying that you have to be, but if you want to, that would be great. But if not, that's okay too," she stumbled over her words, her nervousness evident. Adrian chuckled on the other end of the phone, finding her adorable. "I'm sorry," Amara quickly added, "I'm not really good at this whole talking thing. Honestly, I hate talking on the phone, except with a few people. Most of the time, I end up holding the phone in silence, listening to the other person breathe. It's like we're forcing the conversation, and it becomes overwhelming, so I just end up saying anything." Adrian laughed and reassured her, "That means you should have never been on the phone with them in the first place. Conversations with someone you're attracted to, someone you have a connection with, should never leave you feeling overwhelmed. So, it's not that you're not good at this, maybe it's just that those people weren't good for you." Amara couldn't help but smile and bite her lip as she talked to Adrian. It felt like he knew the perfect words to say. "I just can't get over how easy it is to talk to you. Our conversations earlier in the store, it felt like we've known each other for much longer than just a few hours." Adrian's heart did a little flip at her words. "I feel the same way, Amara. I'm actually very much an introvert. I don't usually approach people I don't know, especially women. But talking to you feels natural, comfortable, you know?" Adrian chuckled, a warm sound that made Amara's heart dance a little. "You know," Amara said, "I've actually been looking forward to this call all day. I mean, I literally kept checking my phone, making sure I didn't miss your call. Pretty lame, right?" Amara laughed, trying to play it off as a joke, but Adrian could sense the truth behind her words. He wanted her to know that her feelings were safe with him. "Amara, you met a man today who felt an unmatched, unexplainable connection with you. A man who spent the rest of his day working, rushing to get home just so he could call you. A man who typed up a text message three or four times, but felt texting was too 'informal' and it might have said I just want to be 'friends' and there's nothing about him that wants to be just friends with you. So, nothing about what you just said is lame. It's flattering, and it means the world to me. I apologize for taking so long, and I assure you it won't happen again." Amara's cheeks blushed on the other end of the phone. Who on earth was this man? "You know, we've talked about me, and I know we touched on you a bit, but tell me more. Do you have any children? Any siblings? Are your parents here in Atlanta too?" Adrian was usually private about his personal life, but there was something about Amara that made him feel comfortable opening up. "No children, but I would love to have some one day. I've always thought if I had a boy, I would make him a Junior, and if I had a girl, I'd name her Trinity Sarai." Amara's upbringing in the church made the name Trinity stand out to her. "Oh wow, I love that! Both names have a biblical connection, right?" Adrian was excited that Amara recognized the significance. "Yes, Trinity to represent the Father, Son, and Holy Spirit, so she knows that God is always with her. And Sarai, to remind her that with God, she can find faithfulness, resilience, and laughter in the face of great odds. No matter the circumstances, God can change them. No matter the gender, age, anything, God can do it." Amara was trying to piece together who this man was – fine, successful, carried himself with confidence, and believed in God. "Adrian, that is amazing and such a beautiful name. It sounds like your parents raised you well." There was a moment of silence, and Amara wasn't sure if she had said something wrong. Then Adrian spoke. "My parents... well, no, my mom and dad didn't play a big role in my upbringing. My mom, my mom, she was, I mean she still is, beautiful. One of the most stunning women you would ever see. Everywhere she went, it looked like she had just stepped off the cover of a magazine. My mom she wasn't a bad person, I honestly just don't believe she was meant to be a mom. I remember the day she knew mom life was just not for her. She picked me up from school, and she told me she was taking me to meet my grandmother. It was her mother, but I had never met her before. She took me to this strange woman's house, but she was my grandmother, so what could I say. She had dropped me off on that Thursday, she told me she loved me, and would see me that Sunday evening. Sunday evening came, but my mother didn't. and I never saw her again. Until this day that was the last day that I physically saw my mother." Amara immediately felt a surge of empathy for Adrian. She thought she had it bad because her mother was dead, but how must it feel to know that your mother is alive, but just didn't want you? "Adrian, I am so sorry you had to experience that." Adrian had worked through his issues regarding his mother, so he was okay. "No apology necessary. Listen, my mother, from what I remember, was an okay mother. She made sure I was fed, clothed, and healthy. I found out later she used to send my grandmother money every week to help with my expenses. Being a mother just wasn't right for her, at the time, I guess. Funny thing is she's married now to some rich guy, she lives in Hilton Head, SC last I checked, and she has two daughters. My grandmother she did her best, she's the one who took me to church, we were there every Wednesday, Saturday, and Sunday. She's the reason God was a part of my upbringing. She passed away when I was fifteen. I ended up in a group home and left when I turned seventeen. I've been on my own ever since." "And what about your dad?" Amara asked, curious to know more. "I never knew my dad growing up, my mother never talked to me about him. A few years back, I had a health scare and needed as much family medical history I could find. I did a little research and found my mom on Facebook. She was going by her middle name now, I saw on her page she was married and had two daughters. I messaged her to call me. She reached out and we talked for a few minutes, enough for me to get what I needed and she also gave me as much information as she had on my pops. I was able to find him, but when I did, I found out he was in prison, serving a thirty-year sentence for murder. He didn't even know my mother had me, apparently he was waiting to be sentenced when he met my mother, he said she never told him anything about me. The crazy thing is, me and him are actually very close. I talk to my pops at least once a week, and I visit him whenever I can. I enjoy spending time with him, learning from him and his mistakes. He made some shitty choices while trying to survive in this world, but he's a good man. A good man who was fighting demons he just didn't know how to slay." Adrian couldn't believe he had just been so open with Amara. The women in his life usually learned about his mother much later. He never shared such intimate details so quickly, but there was something about Amara. Something about the energy she exuded. Adrian knew there was something special about Amara; he just had to put his finger on exactly what it was. Their conversations deepened, revealing layers of vulnerability, and understanding that surpassed the typical boundaries of a first conversation. Amara was in complete awe at how easily Adrian seemed to fit into her world, as if he had always been a part of it. "Wow, it's already 1:30 in the morning. I should probably call it a night; I have a few shoots tomorrow first one is at 10am." Amara said, her voice carrying a subtle yawn. "Time really slipped away didn't it. Hey, Amara, do you have any plans for this Saturday?" Adrian asked, a touch of intrigue in his voice. Amara, with a soft chuckle, replied, "I have a wedding to shoot from 2-6 but afterwards I'm pretty free." "Well, if you aren't too tired, and have a few hours you can spare, I would like to take you out Saturday, it that's ok with you. I head out of town for business on Sunday, and won't be back for a few days, I would like to see you before I leave." He smoothly asked, with a hint of flirtation in his tone. Amara couldn't help but smile on the other end. "Sure, Saturday sounds good." "Perfect, well you get some rest Amara, I will check on you tomorrow." he replied. They both said goodnight. Amara laid in the quiet darkness of her room; her thoughts still wrapped in the warmth of their lengthy conversation. The clock on her bedside table ticked away, marking the passing moments. She couldn't help but replay the sound of Adrian's voice, the laughter they shared, and the subtle excitement that danced through their words. As she started to fall asleep, Amara felt a gentle anticipation for the weekend. Saturday, with its promise of a mysterious plan, lingered in her mind like a whispered secret. Closing her eyes, she let herself drift into dreams, hoping to dream of the amazing man she had met that day. Meanwhile, miles away, Adrian found himself staring at the ceiling, his thoughts echoing the sentiments shared during their phone call. The evening had unfolded so unexpectedly for him. The idea of Saturday was going through his mind. He was already thinking about what he could do to make it a memorable date. As sleep gradually claimed them, there was a story that was about to unfold between Amara and Adrian and neither of them had any idea how amazing it was going to be.

CHAPTER 2

Mesmerized

Adrian's morning started off easy, with sunlight streaming into his room as he got out of bed. Still half-asleep, he shuffled to the kitchen, rubbing his eyes. After a moment, he turned on the coffee machine, and the smell of fresh coffee filled his place. He took a moment to enjoy the warmth of the morning, standing by the window and sipping on his coffee. Outside, the city was waking up, and he could hear the sounds of cars and people. The coffee worked its magic, waking him up and getting him ready for the day. Adrian's phone buzzed, interrupting the quiet of his morning routine. He glanced at the screen, not recognizing the unfamiliar number. With a casual shrug, he answered, his voice a blend of curiosity and caution. "How you doing my boy?" The voice on the other end spoke in a low, intense tone, filled with urgency. "Man, I almost didn't answer you stay getting a new number." "Well, you know, you got to stay as many steps ahead of these folks as possible." The voice on the other end said. "You never call me unless something's wrong. Everything good? Nothing wrong with the chess matches, is it?" Adrian replied, his voice tinged with a hint of suspicion. "Hans Niemann, Adrian" Adrian was silent, he knew Hans Niemann meant someone was stealing form him. He was shocked at the news that someone on his team would even attempt to cross him as such knowing the reputation he had. "Listen Adrian, this one, is a pretty strong threat, that needs to be taken out of the chess match right away. We can't have players in these matches that can't be trusted. Defeats the entire set up of the game. Adrian's grip tightened on the kitchen counter as he absorbed the news. He spent so much time in picking the perfect team, to avoid these possibilities. He knew in the game he was playing that sometimes things got messy. "Where is this weekend's match" Adrian asked. "Florida" the voice informed him. "I was supposed to head down to Nola this weekend, but I think I'ma check in with buddy first. Matter a fact, why don't you meet me at the gym on Sunday let's say about 3. We can link up before the tournament starts." Adrian instructed. Before ending the call, the voice on the other end made sure to tell Adrian "Keep your moves precise, Adrian. We can't afford any weaknesses or vulnerabilities. Think about the strategy and execute. Don't make any stupid moves, ight." The call ended. Adrian couldn't believe it, someone on his team was trying to cheat him out of money. He knew he had created a reputation that demanded he respond to this threat. Adrian also knew who was running his set up out in Florida. It was one of his closes homeboys he started getting money with a while back. They met in the same group home growing up. Adrian had put him on and helped him get his paper up, even put him in a position to run his own city. Adrian was forever loyal to him and couldn't understand why he would back door him like this. Adrian was furious, but knew he had to calm down before he made a decision that could ruin everything. He knew he needed to clear his mind, so he hit up the one person who always helped him think better. His best friend Harrison. Adrian and Harrison had been friends since they were both 17 years old. Harrison was the one person in the world that Adrian trusted more than anybody. He trusted that Harrison with his life. Adrian quickly texted Harrison, "Yo, meet me at the court ASAP. Need to talk." Harrison responded, "Aight, give me about an hour and I'll meet you there? Everything good?" Adrian didn't respond figured he would catch Harrison up when they met at the court. He arrived at the basketball court, seeing Harrison already there, ball in hand. They greeted each other with a dap, a handshake that symbolized their friendship and camaraderie. "Yo, Adrian, you never responded, everything good?" Harrison asked, his voice filled with concern. "You're text seemed urgent. What's goin' on, man?" Adrian took a deep breath, his eyes locked with Harrison's. "Harrison, we got a problem." Harrison with a confused look on his face, "What kind of problem?" Adrian shot a jump shot and said "Trey". We got a problem in Florida." Harrison still not following, "What the fuck Trey got going on?." Adrian took another shot; basketball was how he thought out a lot of is problems. "This motherfucker, apparently trying to make deals behind my back. Using my shit, my product, and making back door deals outside of our fucking territory. On top of that he ain't approaching just anybody, this man making deals with Emilio people. The fuckers that tried to take my empire and kill me. I ain't got all the details I just know he sat down and had an interesting conversation with some of Emilio's people. Word got back, and I got the call this morning. Harrison's face twisted in disbelief. "Damn, for real? That's some foul shit, man. You been looking out for bro since yall was in that damn group home. Damn." Adrian nodded, appreciating Harrison's unwavering support. "Hell yeah, Harrison I let a lot of shit slide you know, to keep the peace. But I can't let this one go. I've put in too much work to let him undermine what I have built and furthermore disrespect me right in my face. This man knows my entire operation, he been rocking with me since the beginning. He knows enough to do actual damage Harrison. I need your guidance on this, because right now, in my mind there's only one option." Harrison dribbled the ball, his eyes focused on Adrian. "Look, man you know I got your back regardless of the decision. I'm riding with you til the wheels fall off no question. What about Emilio though, you think he gone try and start a war behind this shit." Adrian knew how Emilio moved; he was one of the most powerful people to go up against. "I ain't got all the details right now. I'm gone try and set up a sit down with Emilio as soon as we get to Florida. I need to damage control first so he knows this shit ain't coming from me. Then we will figure out the rest." Harrison nodded, "Bet, man listen I'm riding with you. Whatever we got to do, we gone do it together." Adrian felt a renewed sense of determination, knowing he had Harrison by his side. "You right, it got to make sense and I got to make sure the blow back is minimum. As they continued their conversation, Adrian couldn't help but feel grateful for the friendship he shared with Harrison. They had been through a lot together, seen a lot together, their bond was of one of blood brothers. Harrison and Adrian continued their game on the court a friendly one on one game. They both took a break and sat down to lean against the basketball court fence. A smile cam across Adrian's lips as he a name crossed his mind, Amara. In he mist of his frustration he had forget to mention it to Harrison. "Yo, Harrison man I meant to tell you about this girl I met yesterday in the grocery store. Amara." Harrison's eyes widened with curiosity, "Amara huh, lol." Adrian laughed and shook his head. Adrian and Harrison had been friends for years, Harrison knew Adrian like the back of his hand. Adrian never really did relationships. He was very informal and casual with the women he saw. He knew the type of work he did, was easier when you didn't have any vulnerabilities, so he kept most people at a distance. Adrian's voiced filled with a sort of excitement when he spoke about Amara. "Man, she has this beautiful brown skin, locs that flow down her back, beautiful big dark brow eyes. Oh, and her smile, nan Harrison her smile is breathtaking man. And then she got curves in all the right places."

Harrison nodded, a knowing smile forming on his face. "Ok, you seem excited about this one. Where you met her at?" Adrian's smile grew wider as he recalled their first interaction. "It was at the grocery store bruh." Adrian laughed, "The grocery store? So we making love connections in the grocery store now?" Adrian laughed with him, "I know right, of all places. But I mean I saw her and it was like I had to talk to her, I had to say something to her. I introduced myself and we started talking. Before you knew it, we were walking around the store, just vibin'. I don't it felt different, I mean it felt familiar, like I had known her for years." Adrian's eyes lit up as he continued. "We exchanged numbers, and we talked last night on the phone for hours. I don't know it's crazy how comfortable and easy it feels with her. I even told her about my mom and pops. You know I don't tell anyone my personal business. But I mean it just felt like I could talk to her about anything." Harrison grinned, happy for his friend. He knew only a select few people knew about his parents and he knew it wasn't something he would tell a woman so quickly. "That's what's up my boy. I know we play a lot out here, but I don't think anything can match having a good woman by your side. You know we always talk about when you find someone you can vibe with like that, it's rare. Hold on to her, bro. Sounds like she could be a keeper.: Adrian nodded; his heart filled with a mix of excitement. He knew the reason he didn't allow anybody to get close to him was because it created an uncontrollable weakness in his line of work. He knew brining Amara into his world could be dangerous for the both of them. "I hear you bro. I think for now I just want to see where it goes. I'm taking her out Saturday. I'm looking forward to see how it goes." Harrison clapped Adrian on the shoulder while pulling himself off the ground. "I'm happy for you. You deserve someone who brings you peace and brings out the best in you. Just remember, having her in your life creates a weak spot. Keep it quiet as long as you can, date outside the city. You got real enemies out here, be careful." Adrian nodded, appreciating Harrison's words of wisdom and advice. As they continued their conversation, Adrian felt a sense of gratitude for having Harrison as his best friend. They shared not only the challenges of life and work but also the joys and excitement of personal achievements. Adrian knew he had the strength to navigate both worlds, ensuring that he kept personal, and business separate as long as he could.

CHAPTER 3

Blind Faith

Amara sat in the cozy therapy room, her gaze fixed on the floor as she anxiously awaited the start of her session with her therapist, Anna. The room was filled with a sense of safety and understanding, a space where Amara could freely explore her true fears, emotions, and experiences of the past few years. Amara couldn't wait to get to her weekly Friday sessions. Sadrihe had been anticipating talking to her therapist all week to discuss her recent encounter at the grocery store. "Anna, I wish you could have seen him. He was poised, confident, and so attractive. I mean the conversation just flowed effortlessly, like a river. His name is Adrian, and I don't know, there was something special about him. It almost felt like I knew him before, like he was familiar to me. I keep playing our meeting over and over in my head, trying to see if I missed any red flags. He says all the right things, but I can't help but wonder if that's a sign, or if I'm just setting myself up for heartache again." Anna, familiar with Amara's tendency to overthink, listened attentively. "Amara, tell me what's going on. What's on your mind right now?" Amara took a deep breath, her voice filled with vulnerability. "Anna, what if he's like Teagan? What if he's the complete opposite of who I think he is?" Anna understood where Amara's thoughts were heading. "Amara, Adrian is not Marcus. He is a different person, and you are not he same person you were back then." Amara's gaze remained fixed on the floor as she shared her thoughts. "You know, Anna, all I can think about is the day I met Marcus. I was at the AutoZone, trying to buy oil for my car. I was broke, so I didn't have the money for an oil change. I went in to buy a bottle of oil, trying to stretch the 50.00 I had until payday. I didn't know anything about putting oil in my car. I was asking the clerk questions, feeling lost. Then I heard this voice behind me saying, 'Excuse me, sir, put that on my tab and grab two more bottles of oil.' He looked at me and said he would help me. He poured the oil in my car, we exchanged numbers, and if you had asked me then, I would have told you I had met my future husband." Amara closed her eyes, tears welling up. "Eight months later, we were at his house. We ordered pizza, popped some popcorn, and picked up our favorite movie, Love Jones. We were sitting on the couch when my phone rang. It was Denny, a coworker, asking if I could cover his shift the next day. Something came up, and he couldn't make it to work. I told him sure, I could us the extra money. I hung up the phone, and I didn't think much about it. Amara's voice quivered as she recalled the next events, her tears falling freely. "I went to the kitchen to refill out drinks. I remember closing the fridge and turning around, and then BAM! He slapped me. He slapped me so hard that I fell to the ground, and I heard ringing in my ears. My mouth was bleeding, and I didn't know what to do. I was frozen, unable to move. He looked at me, and it was like his eyes turned dark, so evil. I had never seen him like that before. He leaned down, looked me in the eyes and said, 'You belong to me. No man better ever call your phone again. Now cleans all this shit up.' He walked back into the living room, sat down, and continued watching the movie as if nothing had happened. It was like a switch had flipped, and he became an entirely different person, someone I didn't recognize. I hadn't done anything wrong; I hadn't said anything, I had just answered my phone. Amara looked up at Anna, panic evident in her eyes. "What if Adrian is like that? What if he's not who he seems? What if he's capable of hurting women? Maybe I should cancel the date. Maybe I shouldn't go." Anna, prepared for this moment in Amara's healing journey, spoke with conviction. "Amara, Marcus is no longer in your life. He's gone. You have worked so hard to heal yourself, to become better for yourself. You have had amazing progress, and I am incredibly proud of you. You are successful, you are beautiful, and you have learned to recognize red flags. We have discussed the red flags that Marcus displayed, the ones you ignored. Now that you know better, you will never ignore them again. You have created a serene and safe emotional and mental space for yourself, and no one will ever take advantage of you again. You deserve happiness, you deserve peace, and you deserve a good man, Amara. Marcus hurt you because he was fighting his own demons. It was not your fault. He had power over you for years, but you must not allow him to continue having that power. You met an attractive man, and you are going on just one date. Go, have fun, and enjoy yourself. Amara it is safe to find love again. You are doing the work, and you will be okay. Marcus has no power here, not anymore." Amara took a deep breath, feeling a mix of emotions swirl within her. She was a survivor of domestic violence, and she knew firsthand how people could change in an instant. She had been single since her ex, not allowing anyone to get too close for a long time. Something about Adrian felt different, refreshing, but also frightening. As she left her therapy session, Amara felt a renewed sense of strength. Anna was right. She knew the red flags, and this time, she wouldn't dare miss the. She was determined to continue her healing journey, to reclaim her power, and to allow herself the chance to find love again. It was Saturday, and the air in Amara's apartment buzzed with anticipation as she prepared for her night. Standing in front her full length mirror, she marveled at the stunning black dress that hugged her curves, making her feel fierce and unstoppable. The fabric cascaded over her like midnight waves, exuding elegance and allure. Her sister locs framed her face, highlighting her hazel brown eyes. Amara knew she looked amazing, unable to contain her excitement, Amara Face-timed her best friend, Sasha who greeted her with matched enthusiasm. "Look at you, serving looks, honey! If Adrian doesn't take you somewhere fancy, he's missing out big time. You did not come to play," Sasha exclaimed, appreciating Amara's stunning appearance. Amara chuckled, at the delightful exchange of compliments from her best friend. They always made sure to encourage the other at any given time. "You know I have no idea where he's taking me. All I got was a text that said 'be ready by 8' and the dress code is 'dress to impress.' So, I had to turn up the heat a bit," Amara shared, her laughter filling the air. Sasha, always quick with humor, injected her trademark wit. "Make you're your location is on, girl. He might be fine, but we don't know him like that. He could be a serial killer in disguise." Amara and Sasha had a routine of sharing their locations when going out with new acquaintances. As the doorbell chimed, Amara felt a surge of nerves. "Sasha, he's here. I've got to go. Wish me luck." "Good luck girl! Love you! Call me the moment you get home – that's if you don't end up at his place," Sasha teased, their laughter echoing through the phone. "Goodbye, Sasha. Love you even more," Amara replied, beaming with anticipation as she prepared to meet Adrian. As she made her way to the front door, Amara's heart raced with excitement as she opened it to find Adrian standing there, dressed in a sleek black suit that accentuated his charm. His smooth, dark skin glowed in the soft light, and his hair seemed to dance with every step. Gold rope chains adorned his neck, adding a touch of luxury to his ensemble. The fitted blazer showcased his arms, that showed off just how strong he was. Each movement he made exuded confidence, leaving a mark of sophistication. "Good evening," Adrian greeted, a gentle smile playing on his lips. Amara, momentarily speechless, managed a smile in return. "Evening. You clean up well," she replied, her cheeks blushing. "Thank you, and you look amazing, just as I knew you would," Adrian complimented, offering his arm. Amara, feeling a magnetic pull toward him, linked her arm with his. As they walked down the stairs toward the waiting car, Adrian couldn't help but admire how the black dress showcased her confidence and beauty. The night was set to be an adventure, and he was ready for her them both to enjoy the moment. The car glided through the city streets, the soft hum creating a backdrop for their conversation. The city lights twinkled, casting a warm glow on their faces. Adrian guided the conversation with genuine interest, making Amara feel comfortable and engaged. They laughed and shared stories, as if they had known each other for years. The chemistry between them was undeniable, creating a sense of timelessness. Adrian, seated beside Amara, couldn't help but be captivated by the reflection of the city lights in her hazel-brown eyes. The soft fragrance of her perfume added an intimate layer to the moment. Noticing Amara's appreciation for art, Adrian had a surprise in store. The car came to a stop in front of an intimate art gallery, its exterior adorned with a captivating neon glow. Amara's eyes widened with surprise, and she turned toward Adrian with a radiant smile. "You remembered, I love art?" she exclaimed, genuine appreciation in her voice. Adrian grinned, a glint of satisfaction in his eyes. "I pay attention to the things that matter to you." As they stepped out of the car, the evening air kissed their skin, carrying with it the scent of excitement. Inside, soft lighting accentuated the artworks that graced the walls, each piece telling a unique story. Amara, her eyes gleaming with anticipation, wandered through the exhibits, her fingers occasionally grazing the edges of frames. Adrian trailed beside her, observing the spark in her eyes with each new discovery. Approaching a captivating painting, Amara's steps slowed, her gaze fixated on the canvas. "Oh, this is exquisite," she whispered, her voice filled with awe. Adrian, captivated by her appreciation, asked, "What draws you to this one?" Amara's eyes lingered on the artwork, her fingers tracing the contours of an intricate painted embrace. "It's the intimacy, the way the artist captured this moment. It's as if time stands still, and all that exists is this connection between two souls. You can feel the love, the vulnerability. It's raw and beautiful." Adrian leaned in slightly, studying the painting through her eyes. As she spoke, a shared understanding unfolded between them – a silent acknowledgment of the profound emotions embedded in the art. "Love," Amara continued, her voice a gentle melody, "isn't always about grand gestures. Sometimes, it's found in the quiet spaces, in shared glances and unspoken words. This painting encapsulates that essence." Adrian, entranced by her words, nodded in agreement. The gallery became a sacred space where Adrian admired Amara's appreciation for art. Moving from exhibit to exhibit, Amara's insights painted vivid narratives. Their conversation became a dance of intellect and emotion, adding layers to the night and creating a tapestry of shared experiences. As they explored the art gallery, the chemistry between them deepened with every exchanged glance and shared thought. The gallery transformed into a sanctuary where they could be themselves, where their connection blossomed amidst the strokes of pain and the whispers of creativity. After exploring the art gallery, Amara and Adrian stepped out into the cool night air, their hearts still warmed by the shared experience. The city lights cast a soft glow on the streets as they walked hand in hand towards a secluded rooftop bar, offering an uninterrupted view of the skyline. They found a corner table, settling in as the sounds of the city below provided a comforting soundtrack to their conversation. The waiter, skilled in the craft of mixology, concocted signature cocktails that mirrored the vibrant energy of the city. Seated at the rooftop bar, Amara looked at Adrian, her eyes filled with excitement and genuine appreciation. "Adrian, that art gallery was absolutely breathtaking. Each piece seemed to hold a unique story, waiting to be discovered. I truly appreciate the thought and effort you put into tonight." Adrian's face lit up with a warm smile, his gaze fixed on Amara. "I'm so glad you enjoyed it. I wanted tonight to be more than just a typical first date; I wanted it to be an experience that would leave a lasting impression." Amara leaned forward, her hand reaching across the table to touch Adrian's. "Well, you've definitely succeeded. You've exceeded every expectation." As they savored their cocktails, Amara's eyes sparkled with curiosity. She peered over the rim of her glass, eager to continue their conversation and explore the depths of their connection. "May I ask you something?" Adrian, eager to continue getting to know Amara, was open to any questions she had. Amara took a moment to gather her thoughts before speaking. "Your father, you mentioned that he was in prison do you mind me asking what happened?" Adrian was caught off guard by the question, but he wanted to be open with Amara. He never really talked about his family but he wanted to be honest. "My dad he did something I don't event really like to talk about. He was in college back in the day he went to the University of GA" Amara was shocked to hear that "Really my mom went there for a bit. She didn't get to finish but he went." Adrian smiled "Really what a small world. Well yea he went and one night him and his frat buddies got really drunk. Apparently, he was walking home and saw this young woman walking. He tried to spit some game to her and she of course didn't want to be bothered. He um, he attacked her and he umm, he raped her." Adrian sipped his drink, he hated to tell people about his dad in fear of the judgement they might pass. "He was a rapist. After they caught him they were able to tie him to two other rapes that had happen when he was in high school." Amara froze she was taken back by what Adrian had shared with her "Wow. I don't even know what to say really. I can understand why you don't speak about him. I'm so sorry you have to carry that with you now, I hope you don't allow it to hinder you in anyway. You aren't your father." Adrian was surprised by Amara's understanding and empathy. He had shared a vulnerable part of his life with her, and she responded with kindness. "Thank you, Amara. It means a lot to hear you say that." Amara's voice grew softer as she opened up about her own experiences. "Of course, we all have parts of our life that we don't want to talk about. For me it's the fact that I was a man's punching bag for years. I literally lived inside my own hell for most of my life and it continued into my adult life. "Amara, I'm so sorry. I would have never thought..." Amara gently interrupted him, raising her hand to pause his statement. "It's okay, you didn't know. But yes, I was in a really bad situation for five years. At first, I thought he was the love of my life, but then he became someone unrecognizable. It's crazy to think that there were times when others saw how he treated me and said nothing. They just turned a blind eye. Adrian looked at Amara in a whole new light. The poised and delicate woman sitting across from him had endured something incredibly difficult, yet here she was, ready to take on the world. He was even more fascinated by her now and wanted to get to know her even more. Wanting to change the subject and give Amara a break from the heavy emotions, Adrian asked, "Hey, I remember you mentioning that you lived with your father after everything. How was that?" Amara was grateful for the change in topic and didn't want to become too emotional in front of Adrian. "Oh, my dad is amazing. He's truly the best dad ever. Actually, he never knew about the abuse. I hid it from him very well. One thing's for sure, if he had known, he would have done something about it." They both chuckled. "But my dad is awesome. He and my mom didn't work out, mainly due to my mom's mental health struggles. He left when I was about three years old and remarried by the time, I was six. He married my stepmother, who I consider my mom. They've been married for 23 years and will be celebrating their 24th anniversary this year. They weren't able to have children of their own, but my stepmother treated me like she had spent 24 hours in labor with me. I have plenty of uncles and cousins that I love. My dad has five brothers, and my stepmother has three sisters. We're like that TV family, always having big cookouts and celebrating every holiday together. You know, the kind of family that goes all out for Easter, Valentine's Day, St. Patrick's Day, Cinco de Mayo – anything that calls for a big family gathering." Adrian admired the way Amara spoke about her family. He had never experienced that kind of love and togetherness in his own life. Hearing her describe it was pure excitement for him. "That sounds beautiful. Who knows, maybe one day I'll get to meet them." Amara blushed and smiled shyly. "Yeah, I think that might be a possibility." The night continued with shared laughter, lingering glances, and a dance of words that deepened their connection. The city below, with its symphony of lights, mirrored the spark between Amara and Adrian. As they clinked glasses, Amara marveled at the unexpected beauty of the evening. Adrian had planned the perfect date, not just showing her the city and art, but opening a door to a realm where every shared gaze and whispered word felt like a love song. The city skyline stretched before them, a symbol of the boundless possibilities that lay ahead. As they arrived back at Amara's home, hand in hand, the night air caressed them, carrying the distant sounds of conversations and laughter. Standing at her front door, Adrian turned to her with a charming smile, his eyes holding a gentle intensity. "Amara, tonight has been nothing short of incredible. I have to leave town tomorrow for a few business meetings, but I'll be back in a few days. I hope it's okay for me to stay in touch while I'm gone and make plans to see you again when I return." Amara's eyes sparkled with understanding, though a touch of disappointment flickered across her face. "Of course, stay safe, and I'll be expecting your call." “Before I go” Adrian stepped closer, cradling her face in his hands, and pressed his lips to hers in a kiss that ignited a cascade of sensations. It was a slow dance, a fusion of passion and tenderness. Amara felt her knees weaken, her heart racing as if caught in a whirlwind of emotions. Adrian's touch was both electrifying and comforting, a sweet melody that lingered in the air. As they parted, Amara's eyes fluttered open, a dazed smile playing on her lips. Adrian leaned in, whispering, "Goodnight, Amara." Amara, still trying to catch her breath from the intensity of the kiss, replied, "Goodnight, Adrian." With a final lingering gaze, Adrian walked away, leaving Amara standing at her door, her heart pounding and her thoughts consumed by the taste of his kiss. She closed the door behind her, leaning against it, savoring the enchanting residue of a night that had kindled a fire within her soul.

CHAPTER 4

Banished

Adrian pulled up to Harrison's place, his mind focused on the risk that lied ahead of him. As Harrison hopped into the car, he noticed a change in Adrian's demeanor- a seriousness that hinted at a side of him that few had seen. "Adrian, my man, you good?" Adrian's gaze hardened as he turned to Harrison. "Harrison, you know you don't have to go with me right. I can take care of this on my own. You got a family in there man, I ain't trying to jam you up in anyway." Harrison, taken aback by Adrian's response. He had seen a different side of Adrian and knew what he was capable of if you crossed him. He and Adrian had been locked in for years, but never had Adrian offered for Harrison to opt out. "I trust you, Adrian. Whatever it is, I've got your back," Harrison replied, his voice filled with unwavering loyalty. Both of them knew what they were going to Charleston to do but Harrison wanted to ease up the tension a little bit. "Yo, you had that date last night, with ol girl, how did that go?" Adrian smiled glad that Adrian brough up Amara. "Man, it was dope. I can't even lie, I enjoyed myself with her. She's different, I can tell. I haven't known her long I mean not even a week actually but it feels like I'm connected to her already. Shit feel kind of weird. How did you feel the first time you met Monica?" "Shit, the first day I saw her I knew she would be wife. I mean I knew it in the instant, no questions. You know growing up we didn't have the best upbringing, for me it always felt like I was missing something. Like I wasn't some sad ass person walking around like I felt empty, but I always felt there was something I was missing that would make me feel whole. When I saw Monica, it was like instantly I felt like a full person. It was like she was the other half I needed." Adrian smiled, he loved the way Harrison loved his wife and his family, it was something he had always admired about him. "Yea, I never felt anything like this before bruh, that woman got me jonesing really bad. She told me last night her ex used to put his hands on her. Shit had me hot, I already feel like I got to protect her man. When I look at her thought I can't believe she went through something like that. I don't know how I can tell her who I am really am and she still feel saft. She been around dangerous men who hurt her, I don't want her to think I will ever hurt her, but I just don't know if she will be able to see past this shit you know." Adrian breathed out a deep breath. "I'm gone have to tell her eventually, but I plan to show her just how much I'm not like her ex, and regardless of this, I would never put my hands on her. I just got to figure out how to do it the right way." Harrison had never heard his friend talk in this capacity about a woman, but he was happy to hear it. "Man listens if that woman is for you, then it will work. She will see pass this shit and see that you are a good man, my brother. No doubt about that." Harrison and Adrian pounded fist, acknowledgement they were on the same page. "Aight so I set up a sit down with Emilio. First thing first is I need him to know this wasn't me trying to move in on his turf you know. We gone sit down and figure out how to handle both of our people accordingly. The other most important thing is that whatever we decide it doesn't create too much noise, but enough noise so nobody else thinks to play like this again." Adrian and Emilio had crossed paths in the past. Emilio wanted Adrian to work for him, but Adrian was a young motivated, also hot-headed kid. He wanted to work alone and build his own network. Emilio saw him as a threat early on when he watched him hustle his way up. Adrian was very smart and calculated and knew exactly how to become a great in this game. When Adrian was about 21 him and Emilio were at odds. Emilio and Adrian were beefing over territory. There were taking shots at each other, and few of their people were hurt. Adrian knew he was in no position to continue to go to war with Emilio, so they had a sit down. They both came to a mutual agreement, divided up the territory among them and agreed to stay on their own sides. They both had operations going in Florida, but never really needed to talk until now." Harrison and Adrian both needed to get in the best mental head space. Harrison got some shut eye as they drove towards their destination. The car ride was about 5 hours, but they finally reached where they were meeting Emilio. As Adrian and Harrison approached the gate, they couldn't help but be impressed by the sight. The gate was huge, towering above them, with intricate designs that spoke of luxury. Adrian rolled down his window and buzzed in, announcing their arrival. The gate slowly opened, revealing a long driveway lined with beautiful gardens and fountains. Expensive cars were parked in the spacious lot, showing the wealth of the man they were about to meet up with. There were also bodyguards stationed around, a reminder of the seriousness of the situation. Driving up to the front of the house, they saw a man waiting for them at the door. He was dressed in an expensive, tailored suit, and he greeted them with a warm smile. "Welcome, gentlemen," he said, his voice smooth and inviting. "I'm James, Mr. Emilio's personal assistant. Please, come inside." As they entered the mansion, James began to give them a tour. "This house has been in Mr. Emilio's family for generations," he explained. "It has seven bedrooms, each with its own ensuite bathroom. The house is over a century old, and many of its original features have been preserved." Adrian and Harrison were in awe as they walked through the house. The foyer was grand, with a beautiful staircase leading up to the second floor. The walls were adorned with paintings and sculptures, and the floors were covered in plush carpets. James led them into the living room, where they saw a painting that caught their attention. "This painting is from the 18th century," James explained. "It's been in Mr. Emilio's family for generations." Harrison was genuinely impressed by the beauty of the painting. "This is beautiful," he remarked, taking in the artwork with admiration. Adrian nodded in agreement, sharing Harrison's sentiment. "It's definitely something special," he added, appreciating the artistry before them. As James continued the tour, he led them through various rooms of the mansion, showcasing the dining room, kitchen, and library. Each space was more impressive than the last, leaving Adrina and Harrison in awe of the beauty of the house. After the tour, James guided them to a comfortable sitting room, where they settled into plush chairs. "Mr. Emilio will be with you shortly, James informed them, offering refreshments. "Please make yourselves at home." Adrian and Harrison relaxed in their seats, taking a moment to soak in the elegance of their surrounding. The atmosphere was serene, and they awaited the arrival of Mr. Emilio with a sense of anticipation. Moments later, the door swung open, and Emilio entered the room, accompanied by James. "Adrian, Harrison, welcome to my home, one of them," Emilio greeted warmly, extending his hand for a firm handshake, which both Adrian and Harrison reciprocated. "Thank you for agreeing to meet with us," Adrian responded respectfully. "Your home is truly magnificent." Emilio smiled, a glint of pride shining in his eyes. "Let's skip the small talk and address why we're here. We have a common challenge that we need to tackle together." Adrian anticipated Emilio's direct approach. "I agree. I don't have all of the details yet; the information I received was vague. I was informed about some questionable moves being made in our territory, so I cam to gather more information." Emilio, his irritation evident in his tone, stood up from his chair. "Let me fill yo in. That 'cabron' you have overseeing your operations here is attempting to encroach on your territory. He struck a deal with one of my associates behind my back, profiting you're your product and my clientele. We may not always see eye to eye, but in this situation, we must stand untied to send a clear message to anyone thinking of crossing us." Emilio then offered Adrian and Harrison expensive cigars, a gesture of camaraderie. They accepted and lit the cigars as they continued their discussion. Adrian was aware of Emilio's reputation and the depth of his influence, understanding the gravity of the situation they were facing. "Emilio, no disrespect to you or your suggestions, but I think it's best that I handle Trey, and you take care of your own associate. We both know we have different ways of approaching these types of situations, and I would prefer to handle this my way." Emilio reclined in his chair, puffing on his cigar. "Fine. You handle your end, and I'll handle mine. But let me be clear, if I ever encounter Trey in Florida again, he becomes my problem, and well as you stated, you know how I deal with my problems. Clean up your operations Adrian, and I'll do the same. Agreed?" Adrian understood the seriousness of Emilio's words. While Emilio's tactics didn't intimidate him, he was aware of the stories surrounding Emilio and how ruthless he could be. Despite Trey's actions, Adrian was mindful of potential collateral damage and assured Emilio that Trey would not be seen in Florida again.

CHAPTER 5

In The Shadows

Amara's cozy living room provided the perfect space for her long-overdue catch up with her bestie Sasha. The clinking of glasses and the harmonious laughter of two friends rung through the room as they settled into the plush couch. "Girl, where have you been hiding? I swear, it feels like a century since we last caught up!" Sasha exclaimed, taking a sip of her drink. Amara chuckled, "Oh, you know how it is hustling hard and stacking those coins. The photography gig has been blowing up lately." Sasha always happy to hear about her friends accomplishments, "Yes mam, I am so proud of you sis. You put in the work and now it is paying off. Glasses up to being booked and busy." They clinked their glasses together again. Sasha raised an eyebrow, a mischievous glimmer dancing in her eyes. "So, I haven't really talked to you since you were getting ready for your hot date. So dish the dirt, honey! How was it, don't skip any details." Amara blushed, a shy smile playing on her lips. "Oh, Sasha, he's something else. Our date was like a scene from a romance movie, and I can't get him out of mind." Leaning in with eager anticipation, Sasha urged, "Spill the tea, girl! Where did yall go? What did he plan, oh my goodness, give me all the deets!" Amara was excited to share the experience she had with Adrina that night. “Girl, he took me to this art exhibit, and it was amazing. There were so many great pieces of art there I loved it. After we had dinner on a rooftop over looking the city. We talked for hours and hours and I don’t know it was so effortless. Like I can’t remember a time when it was easy to talk to a man the way it is to talk to him.” As Amara continued to share the worthy moments from the date, Sasha erupted into laughter, clapping her hands in excitement. “Girl, you’ve got yourself a keeper! This sounds like the real deal. I’m telling you, this could the be the one Amara, OMG!” Amara smirked, “Let’s not get ahead of ourselves. It’s still early days, but he’s definitely piqued my interest.” Amara looked down at her glass, Sasha could tell something was on Amara’s mind. “Ok, what’s going on here, what’s that look?” Amara took a deep breath, “I don’t know, but you remember, I felt like this when I met Tegan. I thought he was the best man; I had ever met. I remember us having this exact same conversation back then. We said, ‘he’s the one’ and he turned out to be the one who destroyed me. He broke me in ways I haven’t learned to describe in words yet. I just can’t help but think or wonder what if Adrian isn’t who he seems to be. What if he’s like Teagan and abusive?” Sasha stood up waving her arms, “No, no, no. Hell no. We are not doing this today. That man took years from you, he made you feel worthless, unloved, and he stole something from you. You have worked your ass off to get all of that back, and I be damned if he is going to steal this away from you again. That man was the devil, and he was only meant to kill and destroy and that’s what he tried to do to you. But you stood up and took your joy back, your smile back, your happiness back! I will not watch you throw away your life because of that asshole. Adrian is not Tegan.” Amara knew Sasha was right, she just couldn’t help get into her own head. Their conversation smoothly transitioned from dating escapades to work talk, from giggles to heartfelt conversations about life’s twists and turns. Amara cherished these moments, where she could bare her soul to a friend who truly understood her journey. Amara and Sasha continued to chatter away their laughter filling the room with warmth and joy. Amara's phone buzzed on the coffee table, displaying Adrian's name. Shooting Sasha a mischievous grin, Amara answered the call, her voice laced with playful intrigue. "Hey, handsome," Amara purred into the phone, a hint of playfulness in her tone. "To what do I owe the pleasure of this late-night call?" Adrian's velvety voice flowed through the line, "Hey, beautiful. I actually am just getting in and settled. I could not resist hearing your sweet voice. How's your night shaping up?" Amara reclined, twirling a lock of her hair between her fingers. "Just hanging out with my girl Sasha, catching up. How about you?" Adrian chuckled, "Oh you know, the usual grind. My apologies I haven't called sooner. My business trip went a little longer than anticipated. A two day trip turned into a week. My business partners kept me so busy, I didn't have much time to sit and talk. But thoughts of our date kept sneaking into my mind. And the vision of you that night...mesmerizing. So I wanted to call and check in before I hit the hay. Maybe see if you were up for a little mischief this Saturday night?" Amara couldn't help but blush as the compliment. "Aren't you a smooth talker. What kind of mischief are we talking about?" Adrian's voice took on a seductive edge, "How about you just be ready at 7pm, and I will send a car for you. What do you say?" Amara's heart danced with excitement. "Mmm, you are something else Mr. Bishop. Yes, I would love to join you and I will be ready Saturday at 7." The call left Amara with a satisfied grin, eagerly anticipating the weekend. Glancing at Sasha, who was grinning mischievously, Amara shared the news,: Looks like I've got another hot date lined up for the weekend!" Sasha burst into laughter, "Girl, I love this so much for you! Look at the smile on your face. This man is working wonders on you, and I am here for it! He is not Teagan. Be happy Amara, don't let that man take anything from else from you. Ok?" Amara's eyes sparkled with a mix of excitement and wonder. "You're right girl, he is not Teagan. Adrian is confident, a tad mysterious, but so genuine. And those eyes, Sasha. It's like they see right through me. When he looks at me, it's like he's peeling back layers I didn't even know I had. I feel seen, like truly seen, in a way I've never experienced before." Raising her glass, Sasha proposed a toast, "Well, here's to whatever this is! As long as it's bringing you joy, I'm all in. To new beginnings and good vibes!" Amara clinked her glass with Sasha's, both taking a sip. "Cheers! And yes, to happiness, love, and the thrilling adventure with Adrian. I'm ready for it all." They shared a few more laughs and clinks, celebrating the unpredictability of love and the promise of something extraordinary in Amra's life. As the soft evening light filled her apartment, Amara stood in front of her closet, trying to decide what to wear for her date with Adrian. She felt a mix of excitement and nervousness about the evening. After thinking it over, she picked out a stylish jumpsuit in earthy tones that hugged her figure nicely. The fabric shimmered in the light, making her feel confident and chic. Looking at herself in the mirror, she felt good about her choice. As the time for the car to arrive drew closer, her phone buzzed with a message. She figured it was Adrian letting her know the car was about to arrive. But to her surprise the text from an unknown number. When she opened the text she saw a photo of herself taken from outside her window while she was getting dressed. It made her feel uneasy, someone had to be watching her. The message that came with the photo was strange and unsettling. It read "In the shadows, your secrets lie. Beware the eyes that watch without seeing." The words sent a chill down her spine. Leaving her feeling on edge. As the car pulled up outside her home, Amara felt a surge of nervous energy knotting in her stomach. She hesitated for a moment, her hand hovering over the doorknob, a flicker of uncertainty clouding her mind. The cryptic message and unsettling photo from earlier lingered in her thoughts, casting a shadow of doubt over the evening ahead. Steeling herself, Amara took a deep breath and stepped out into the cool evening air. The driver greeted her warmly, but her mind was elsewhere, consumed by the mystery that had unfolded in her own home. As they arrived at the venue, Amara found herself torn. Should she confide in Adrian about the strange message and her suspicions or keep it to herself. The thought of her abusive ex crossed her mind, a chilling reminder of a past she had fought to leave behind. She couldn't stop thinking about the very last thing her ex said to her, "I'll never stop loving you Amara! Never!" Amara decided she wouldn't mention any of this to Adrian. She didn't want to scare him off. She decided she would handle this situation herself later and get to the bottom of it. As she stepped out of the car and into the warm glow of a beautiful restaurant, Amara plastered a smile on her face, pushing aside her worries for the time being. The evening with Adrian awaited, and she was determined to enjoy it, all the while keeping a watchful eye on the shadows that seemed to follow her every move.

CHAPTER 6

Baggage

The next morning Amara awoke thinking about the date her and Adrian had the night before. She had a great time with him, and truly enjoyed spending time with Adrina. She had to work the next morning, so she didn't stay out to late. Plus, she couldn't get her mind of that text message she had gotten yesterday. She decided not to tell Adrian and figured when time permitted, she would look into it herself. But today was a day where she got to make photographic magic for her clients. She got up and got dressed ready for an amazing day. The wedding venue buzzed with love and laughter as Amara captured precious moments with her camera. The joy on the bride's face and the groom's adoring gaze were frozen in time with each click of her shutter, creating memories to cherish forever. As the night went on, Amara moved seamlessly between capturing candid shots and intimate portraits, the love and happiness of the newlyweds and their guests filling her heart. However, beneath all of the love and celebration, that uneasy feeling was still lingering in her mind. The night was winding down and it was time for Amara to begin packing up her gear at the end of the night. Amara went to open her bag to put her things away, and she found an envelope hiding inside. Amara looked around as she knew the envelope was not in her bag when she left home. Amara nervously took the envelope out of her bag and opened it. What she found immediately sent chills down her spine. She found pictures of her and Adrian from their date last night. There were photos of them eating, talking, and kissing. There was over 20 photos of them from the night before and a letter. Amara was really freaked out now. She opened the letter and it read 'In the shadows, unseen eyes watch your every move. Beware the company you keep, for not all who stand beside you are allies. Collateral damage is a cruel fate for those who stray from the path of caution. The veil of mystery shrouds your steps, a warning whispered on the winds of time. The dance of shadows and light reveals truths that may haunt the unwary. The eyes that watch see more than you know. In the garden of your thoughts, plant seeds of suspicion and water them with the dew of distrust. The moon's gentle light may guide you, but darkness lurks in the corners, waiting to ensnare the unsuspecting. Trust not in the mirror's reflection, for illusions cloud the truth. Listen to the whispers of caution, for they may save you from the abyss. The journey ahead is treacherous; tread carefully, lest you become a casualty of the shadows. Signed Yours in warning, A watcher in the Dark.' Amara's heart raced as she scanned the room, her eyes darting from one face to another, searching for any signs of suspicion. The fear that gripped her was undeniable, the sense of being watched sending a chill down her spine. She couldn't shake the feeling that her ex was behind this, a shadow from her past haunter her present. With trembling hands, she grabbed her phone and composed a message to Sasha, her fingers tapping out a plea for help and comfort. The urgency in her words reflected the depth of her unease. As she made her way to her car, the phone call from Adrian pierced through the silence, a reminder of the complexities of her situation Amara hesitated, she knew if she answered Adrian would hear the uneasy shaking in her voice. She wanted to talk to Sasha first before she spoke to Adrian. The drive to Saha's was a blur. Amara arrived to Sasha's doorstep, her nerves on edge, the events of the past days playing out like a haunting melody in her mind. She knocked on her best friends door, her heart racing with a mix of anxiety and anticipation. She needed to talk to her trusted friend, she needed help to try and figure out what to do next. As Amara stepped into Sasha's cozy living room, the familiar scent of home and he warmth of her friend's embrace provided a much-needed diversion from the chaos swirling in her mind. Sasha's eyes widened in concern as she ushered Amara to the couch, a mix of worry and determination etched on her face. "Amara are you ok what the hell is going on. It's 8pm on a Sunday night and you looking like you seen a ghost." Amara didn't answer Sasha right away, she went straight to the kitchen to her friends liquor cabinet, grabbed a bottle of crown apple and poured herself a double shot. She needed a second to breath before she told her friend about the suspicious activity she had encountered. Amara took a double shot and then looked at her confused best friend. "Somebody's watching me Sasha, and I think it's Teagan." Sasha had a look of confusion on her face, "Watching you? What are you talking about Amara?" Amara poured another drink and threw it back. "Ok, Saturday night right I was getting dressed for my date with Adrian. And I got a text, see look." Amara showed Sasha the text she received Saturday night. "What the fuck, who is this from?" "I don't know it came from an unknown number." Sasha slightly concerned; did you tell Adrian about it?" "No, I didn't know what it was, I mean I didn't want him to think I got all this crazy people drama around me you know. So I didn't mention it to him." Sasha poured another drink and looked at Sasha, "That's not all." Amara handed Sasha the envelope that was left in her bag at the wedding. Sasha's eyes widened as she took the envelope, her brows furrowed in concern as she examined the contents. The phots, and the letter. "Damn, Amara. Someone really is watching you. This is some serious shit. We have to tell someone; we need to go to the police." Amara shook her head, a mix of fear and determination in her gaze as she met Sasha's eyes. "No, not yet. Sasha this has to be Teagan. Who else would do something like this? I can't go to the police if it's him. You remember what he did to me that time I called the cops. I can't risk it. I don't know what to do." Sasha's voice filled with compassion, her hand squeezing Amara's in a gesture of unwavering support. "Ok, fine if you don't want to go to the police, we can figure it out together. Don't you think you should at least tell Adrian?" Amara shook her head "No, I don't want him to know anything. Adrina doesn't know about Teagan, the therapy none of that. He already knows my mother killed herself, I don't want him to think I'm so drama filled basket case. I don't want to tell anyone right now. I just want to try to figure out what the hell is going on first, and if it is Teagan." Sasha didn't agree with her friend, but she understood. Teagan was the boogey man of her best friends' stories. She knew how much he frightened Amara, and she didn't want to scare her anymore than she already was. "Ok, why don't we do this, why don't you stay here with me tonight. I will be up for a while I have to finish answering some emails and finish my proposal for my boss. You go upstairs shower and lay down. I'll keep watch down here so you can rest peacefully ok." Amara knew her best friend would aways have her back. Sasha was always there for Amara. Amara was grateful to have a friend like Sasha. She knew together they would figure out what was going on and get to the bottom of it. Amar went upstairs to take a shower she knew she needed to do her best to try and get some rest. She hadn't really slept since she got the first text that Saturday. Amara showered and laid in her best friend's bed. Sasha always had the comfiest bed it felt as though she was laying on a cloud. Amara slowly drifted off into sleep. "Teagan stop please!" Amara screamed as she ran through the apartment trying to stop her boyfriend from attacking her.

"Naw, who the fuck was that calling your phone?" Teagan screamed as he grabbed Amara's hair, dragging her from their bedroom and down the stairs. "I told you not to have men calling your phone!" Bam! Bam! Teagan was slapping Amara in her face while she was screaming for help. "Teagan he's my boss, he just wanted to see if I could work tomorrow." Amara was able to get to her feet and ran into the kitchen. Teagan followed behind her and when she turned around there he was and he started to choke her. Amara couldn't breath, she started to slap Teagan's hands attempting to make him let her go. Teagan stared into her eyes and said "I will kill you before I ever let you leave me." Amara scared for her life, was able to grab a knife, and she cut Teagan's arm. Teagan let her go and Amara took off. Only in a t-shirt and panties she sprinted out the back door and down the hill to a neighbors house. She was screaming "Call the police, call the police. He's trying to kill me." Amara finally made it to her neighbors house, she was banging on the door for help. The door finally opened and on the other end of the door was Teagan. He laughed and said "Welcome Home!" Thump! Amara hit the floor. She looked around panting and sweating and realized she had woken up from a nightmare. She looked at the clock on the night stand it was 6:43am. She knew Sasha was probably downstairs getting ready to leave for work. She knew she needed to head home and get herself together. She had just had a nightmare that she hadn't had in such a long time. Amara felt like she was back in a place that she worked so hard to get out of. She had to figure out if it was truly Teagan behind the anonymous contact. She still didn't want to tell Adrian everything but figured she should talk to him and tell him everything about her past relationship. She checked her phone and saw she had 14 missed calls and 22 text messages, all from Adrian. He had been trying to reach her and was worried something had happen to her. She felt so bad for ignoring Adrian, but she needed a few hours to just get her head space together. She sent him a text

'Hey, there's somethings you should know. Can you meet me at the Café around the corner from my house in an hour?" Amara sent the text and got an immediate response 'Are you ok?' It made her smile that Adrian's main concern was her safety. This made her feel even more confident that letting him in was the right thing to do. 'I'm ok. I will talk to you in person if that's ok.' Adrian responded back right away 'See you at 8.' Amara made her way down the hallway and she could smell the coffee brewing in the kitchen. "Good Morning Sasha." Sasha was sitting at the kitchen island on her computer drinking a cup of coffee. "Hey sis. How'd you sleep?" Amara knew she was exhausted form having that dream. "I dreamed about Teagan last night, so not so good.' Sasha could see her friend was struggling and she wish there was more she could do for her. "Listen, we don't even know if this is Teagan. I mean you do have a new man in your life, how do you know it doesn't have something to do with Adrian? Or maybe we could go to the police and let them figure it out and get you some protection." Amara didn't have much trust when it came to the police. When Teagan first put his hands on Amara she fought him back. She did everything she could to defend herself. She was finally able to call the cops and they came to the house. When they arrived Amara told them that Teagan had attacked her. Teagan lied to the police and told them Amara had caught him cheating and she attacked him first. He lied and said that him hitting her was his only way to defend himself before she killed him. Teagan told the cops that if Amara wanted to press charges so did, he. The police told Amara that they could charge the both of them and then the courts would decide who was truly responsible. Amara couldn't believe it. She had just been beaten by the man she loved and the police were telling her by reporting her abuse she could also be arrested. Amara didn't press charges that day, and the beatings got worse after. She lost all of her trust in the cops that day and figured she was better off figuring out who this person was on her own. "Sasha, you know how I feel about the cops. I'm going to figure this one out on my own. I'm going to head home and shower then meet Adrian for a coffee. I'm not going to tell him about the recent pictures but I am going to tell him about Teagan, and what that relationship did to me. I think it's important he knows before he decides if he really wants to keep pursuing this, you know." Sasha agreed with Amara. "I agree sis. Well, I am about to head out I have to go into the office. Do me a favor lock up and set the alarm on your way out please. I love you, text me or call me if you need me today ok." Amara was so thankful to have a friend like Sasha. "Ok, Sash. Love you more." Amara arrived at the coffee shop around the corner of her house and Adrian was sitting there waiting for her. He saw Amara and immediately hugged her out of concern, and worry from the night before. "Amara I was worried sick about you. Are you sure you're ok?" Amara smiled, "Yes, I'm ok. I was just having a moment yesterday. There's something I need to tell you about my past relationship that you should know. It has a major impact on my current present self now so I think you knowing would help a lot." Adrian was curious and also worried about Amara was going to tell him. Was it something that was going to make him not want to continue with her? "Ok, the floors yours Amara." Amara took a deep breath and she let it go "His name was Teagan. I met him young, and I thought he would be the love of my life. I had, had a few relationships before him, but it was my first real relationship. I didn't get the guys in school or anything like that, so when he came and showered me in compliments and love I felt beautiful and more loved than I ever had before." Sasha closed her eyes and continued to recall her past with Teagan. "I had the same number for years you know. One day we were sitting at his place and my phone rang. I saw the caller ID and knew it was an ex boyfriend from years ago. I hadn't talk to him in over 3 or 4 years, so when I saw him call I didn't think anything of it. Figured I would just tell him I had a boyfriend and that would be it. But when I answered that phone, and Teagan heard a guy's voice on the other end it was like all of the light in his eyes left, and all I saw was darkness. I remember he jerked the phone out of my hand and started screaming and cursing into the phone, he broke it in half and threw it across the room. I had seen him yell before, but I had never seen him like this. It was like another person entered his body and I didn't even recognize him." Adrian sat at the table listening to Amara attentively. He was taken back by what he was hearing about Amara's past relationship. "He started to scream at me asking who the guy was an I was trying to explain it to him, but then it happened. The one thing I never would have imagined he would do. He slapped me so hard that I flew into he corner of the wall. He picked me up by my throat and started chocking me. I was begging for him to stop, begging him not to kill me. When he finally let go, I remember falling to the floor coughing and gasping for air. I was terrified. I got up and ran into the bathroom to get away from him. He had busted my lips and I was bleeding from my mouth. I should have left that day. I should have got my shit and ran for my life. But I didn't. I cleaned myself up, got in the shower and cried in silence. I got out the shower and got right into bed with him." Amara had tears streaming down her face. Recounting the past was hard for her to do but she knew Adrian needed to know. "He told me it was an accident and it would never happen again. So I stayed, but things only got worse. The beatings got worse and worse and eventually I was isolated form everyone. I started to have days that I didn't want to get out of bed. I got to a point where I didn't even want to go to work or be around anyone. I felt heavy, like there was something pressing on my shoulders, something was weighing me down. I felt sad, I was constantly tired, I cried every day in silence. I felt like the entire world was so far away from me. It felt like everyone I knew was on a different planet, and I was all alone. Screaming for help, waving my hands for someone to come save me. But not realizing my screams were silent. No one could hear me, no one saw me, and I felt like no one was coming to save me." Amara took a sip of water she was getting chocked up telling her story to Adrian. "He broke me in a way I didn't think as possible, and I'm putting a few pieces back together. After being in such a traumatic situation you have to expect I suffer from some mental health concerns now. Severe anxiety, PTSD, as well as bipolar depression. I go to therapy weekly, and I am taking some meds that helps keep me leveled." Amara looked at Adrian figuring she had for sure scared him off. Adrian was looking at Amara with concern and sadness in his eyes. He couldn't believe the woman he was sitting across from him went through something so painful. He wanted to grab her and just hold her in his arms. "Amara, I am so sorry that you had to experience that at the hands of someone you loved. I had no idea" Amara waved her hand for him to stop, "Of course you didn't, it's not something I share with many people. It's a part of my life I like to keep private if I can. But the past few days I've been having nightmares, reliving some of the altercations we had. That's why I've been so distant. I haven't dated anyone since him, and it's not that you are like him or anything it's just, my anxiety was getting the best of me. Adrian wanted to assure Amara that he was nothing like her ex. Adrian knew he was hiding something from Amara but it was nothing of that magnitude. "Amara, listen I understand your worry and I would honestly be worried too. I could sit here and tell you I'm nothing like your ex, I would never do anything to intentionally hurt you, and I would never ever put my hands on you. But, I also know words don't always carry much weight with someone who has endured what you have. I just hope you allow me to show you that I'm different. I will use my days to protect your heart, not hurt it. I will help you finish putting all the pieces back together. Amara I'm asking you to trust me. I know that might be hard for you to do, but if you give me a chance, a real chance I will prove it to you. Amara was happy to hear that she hadn't scared Adrian off. She didn't tell him about the recent anonymous messages. She figured if he knew there was still some kind of drama going on he would either try to get her to contact the police, or he would truly walk away. She had shared enough with him for now, and she was happy with the way he responded. She couldn't believe Adrian was this amazing. She was in complete awe of him. "Adrian what are you doing this weekend?" Adrian smiled at the excitement of Amara possibly asking him out. "I have a few things to take care of with work, but other than that not too much." "My parents, my dad and step mom are having a big cookout. It's my step moms birthday. I wanted to know if you wanted to join me?" Adrian's smile stretched across his face. "I would love to meet your family baby." Amara breathed a breath of relief. She knew her entire family would be there including Sasha. They had heard about Adrian but she figured it was time they met the mystery man. Amara and Adrian finished their breakfast. Adrian had a few business meetings so he kissed Amara goodbye and told her he would check on her in a few hours. Amara felt such a sense of release. She had shared her toughest traumatic memory with Adrian, and she felt good about it. She was falling for Adrian hard, she hoped her family would love him.

CHAPTER 7

The Cookout

The sun hung lazily in the late afternoon sky as Amara and Adrian made their way to the family gathering at her parent's home. As Amara and Adrian approached, the air was filled with the mouth-watering smell of sizzling barbecue, and delicious foods. Sasha, was already in the midst of lively banter with Amara's cousins, wielding a spatula like a seasoned grill master. "Look who finally decided to show up!" Sasha teased, her eyes dancing with playful mischief as Amara and Adrian joined the festivities. "Traffic, blame it on the traffic," Adrian chuckled, his easygoing charm, effortlessly breaking the ice. Amara grinned, playfully nudging Sasha. "Sasha, meet the man who's been keeping me on my toes – Adrian. Adrian, this is the infamous Sasha." Sasha extended her arms and embraced Adrian in a hug. "So, you're the one who has my best friend grinning from ear to ear." Adrian laughed, "I do my best, you know putting a smile on her face is one of my daily goals. Sasha smiled hard and looked at Amara. "Yes mam, ok I love it. I love all of this for you. So, Adrian, spill the beans. Amara can be a handful. How are you holding up brother?" Sasha probed, her eyes twinkling with curiosity as she nudged Amara. Adrian shot Amara a look of excitement, "Let's just say she makes life, easy. She makes everything easy." Sasha raised an eyebrow, happy to hear about a man who spoke so highly of her best friend. "Easy? You must really like her." Adrian's response was accompanied by a sly grin, "Sometimes, I'm not even sure if like is the words that describes it." Amara looked at Adrian with a shy grin on her face. She knew she felt like she had strong feelings for Adrian. She felt like she loved him, but figured it was too soon to say. Amara was happy to hear that she wasn't the only one feeling something stronger between the two of them. Amara led Adrian through the lively backyard, you could hear her family laughing and the old school music blasting from the speakers. Amara and Adrian made their way to the grill, as they approached the grill, Amara gave Adrian a reassuring smile. "My dad loves his grill time. Just be yourself he is going to he's an easy person to talk to." Jamal, a seasoned grill master with a spatula in hand, turned at the sound of their approach. Amara nudged Adrian forward. "Hey daddy" Amara said while embracing her father. "Hey baby girl, how you doing?" Amara's dad said as he embraced her back. "I'm good dad, you looking good too. I see mom is keeping you in that gym." Jamal laughed "Well you know, your mom is still one fine ass woman, I got to keep up with her." They both laughed, Amara knew this was a great time to introduce her dad to Adrian. "Dad this is Adrian. Adrian, meet the Grill King himself my dad Jamal." Jamal set down the spatula and extended a hand, a friendly smile on his face. "Adrian, good to finally meet you. Amaras told us great things about you. She has been keeping you hidden for too long. Good to finally meet you my man." Adrian chuckled, shaking Jamal's hand. "I've been looking forward to this, sir. I've heard great things about you as well. Amara told me you're the man when it comes to grilling. I'm dying to try to the famous rib sauce." Jamal laughed heartily. "Son, I might tell you a joke, but I won't tell you a lie, I'm the grill master around here. Can't nobody make rib sauce better than me. You know, the secret is all in the seasoning. You stick around long enough I can teach you a thing or two." Amara knew here dad had no filter and would say the first thing on his mind. "Alright, Dad, where's Mom? I don't see her," Amara chimed in, her gaze shifting toward the house. Jamal, Amara's dad, turned towards the house, a knowing smile on his face. "She's in the kitchen, baby, with your aunts. Now Adrian, you're about to walk into the den of wolves in there. They not as nice as me, they gone grill you down. Take no offense it's love. We just real protective over our baby girl. But, I hope you're ready," he said, chuckling. Adrian took a deep breath, a playful glint in his eye. "Wolves, huh? Any advice." "Yea, run. Naw I'm kidding you'll be fine." Laughter and the aroma of grilled goodness filled the air as Amara led Adrian into the house. The kitchen, was buzzing with music and laughter as Amara's step mom, Evelyn, and her aunts, Vanessa and Rose. "Hey Ma" Amara said as she hugged her step mother. "Hey baby girl how are you?" "I'm good. Hey aunt Vanessa, aunt Rose, how are the two of you?" They hugged their niece "Hey baby, we good. It's good to see you. Um, Amara who is this fine young man with you?" Her aunt asked as she looked at Adrian over Amara's shoulder. "Mom, aunties say hello to my boyfriend, Adrian." Evelyn turned, a welcoming smile lighting up her face as she wiped her hands on a kitchen towel. "Well, well, the mysterious Adrian. My daughter has told me so much about you. It's so nice to meet you baby. I'm Evelyn, I'm Amara's step mom." Adrian hugged Amara's mom "Pleasure to finally meet you, Mrs. Evelyn." Amara's Aunt Vanessa, gave Adrian a playful wink. "Oh, aren't you a handsome one? Amara, why you hiding' this eye candy from us?" Amara rolled her eyes, laughing. "Aunt Vanessa, please. Adrian, meet my aunt Vanessa—resident flirt and jokester." Adrian chuckled, feeling right at home. "Nice to meet you, aunt Vanessa. Amara must get some of her looks from you." Vanessa laughed, giving Amara a teasing look. "Amara, you've been holdin' out on us. You did good niecy!" Amara playfully nudged Adrian.

"See what I have to deal with Adrian. My sister in laws are crazy. Evelyn's eyes sparkled with warmth as she regarded Adrian. "Now, tell me about yourself, Adrian. Where you from? What do you do?" Adrian smiled, appreciating the genuine interest. "I'm originally from Atlanta and I work in real estate. I've been doing real estate for about 10 years now." Evelyn settled into a chair, sipping her sweet tea, her eyes keenly fixed on Adrian. "What made you venture into real estate?" Adrian leaned back, feeling the genuine interest in her gaze. "Well, I've always been fascinated in helping people make their dreams come true. There's something about helping someone find their dream home that feels incredibly rewarding. And it allows me to be my own boss, which I love as well." Evelyn nodded, a thoughtful expression on her face. "I like that you say you do your job to help others smile. That truly sounds rewarding. Now, tell me, what are your intentions with my daughter? Amara has been through a lot and she is my world. I have to make sure she is in good hands, because she hasn't always been in the past. Adrian met Evelyn's gaze with sincerity. He knew that she was hinting to the past abusive relationship Amara was in. He wanted to assure her mother he was not the same type of person. "Your daughter is amazing, and I can't understand why or how anyone could hurt someone so beautiful and delicate. When I look at Amara I see someone I can have a future with. I see someone I can build something with. She is sweet, kind, and heartless. I've never met someone like Amara before in my entire life. I'm willing to change the weather behind this woman Mrs. Evelyn." Evelyn smiled, "That's what I like to hear. Amara has had her fair share of unfairness in this world, she deserves some real love and peace. Now, tell me about your family. Are they here in Atlanta too?" Adrian didn't mind sharing his personal life with Amara's family he could tell they were good and genuine people. "I'm actually not close with my family. My mother didn't raise me, my grandmother did. And my father, well my father is serving a life sentence in prison. My grandmother passed away when I was a teenager and I've been on my own ever since. Amara's stepmother looked at Adrian with caring eyes, "Oh Adrian, I am so sorry to hear that. Family is so important, I am sorry you didn't get to experience that fully. But lucky for you, you've met Amara. And her family has enough love to share with everyone." Adrian smiled, just to hear "Mrs. Evelyn, I hope you don't mind but I wanted to get you a little something, a small token of appreciation for welcoming me into your home," Adrian said, holding out the elegantly wrapped gift. Evelyn, touched by his gesture, smiled warmly. "Oh, Adrian, you really didn't have to. But thank you, that's so thoughtful of you." As she unwrapped the gift, Evelyn's eyes widened with surprise and delight. The sunlight caught the sparkle of the intricate elephant pendant, and she gasped in amazement. "Oh, my goodness! Adrian, this is beautiful! Elephants are my absolute favorite. Adrian nodded, pleased to have chosen a gift that resonated with her. "I'm glad you like it, Mrs. Evelyn. Amara told me how much you loved elephants. Amara observed from a distance as Adrian presented her mother with the carefully chosen gift. The sight of her mother's radiant smile, warmed Amara's heart. In that moment, Amara reflected on how lucky she was to have someone like Adrian in her life. His thoughtfulness, kindness, and genuine connection with her family were qualities that went beyond the surface of a typical romantic relationship. Adrian excused himself from the lively gathering, indicating to Amara that he was heading outside to join the guys and have a chat with her father. As he stepped into the backyard, he found Jamal tending to the barbecue, he could tell it was the man's pride and joy. "Hey, Mr. Jamal, mind if I join you for a minute?" Adrian approached, a warm smile on his face. Jamal grinned, extending a hand. "Call me Jamal, young man. No need for the 'Mr.' stuff. Want a beer?" "Sure," Adrian took the beer and sat down on the table next to Jamal. "Just wanted to catch a moment with you if that's alright."

Jamal raised an eyebrow, his eyes gleaming with curiosity. "Well, hey you got my time right now son, what's on your mind?" Adrian took a deep breath, he knew he had only knew Amar for a little while but he knew he loved her already. Since meeting Amara, Adrian knew he would marry her, he had purchased the ring after their third date. "I wanted to talk to you about your daughter. Amara is an incredible woman. She's strong, resilient, and truly brave. She has endured some tough things over her life. She makes no excuses for who she is and she is true to that. I know I've only known your daughter for some time, and it may seem like this is too soon. But I love Amara and I want to ask her to marry me." "Love," Jamal turned around grabbed a bear and sat down next to Adrian. "That is one powerful word. Um, stronger than any drug you can get out on these streets' son, you know that. You get the right hit, one time, and your stuck for life. I remember when I met my Evelyn. I had already had Amara with her mom, but me and her didn't work out. I was a single man, and it was the summertime, summer of '88," Jamal began, a nostalgic twinkle in his eye. "Evelyn and I met at a neighborhood block party. She was something else, a vision in a floral dress and a smile that could light up the darkest room. I remember walking up to her nervous as could be. I had never seen a woman so beautiful in my life. I asked her to dance and man we danced all night long. I remember going home and I called my mother. I said Ma, I want to tell you something, I met my wife tonight. 20 years later and here I am. I couldn't imagine going through my days without that woman in my life. But love, son, it's more than just a feeling. It's a choice, a commitment to stand by someone through thick and thin," Jamal continued, his voice carrying the weight of years of wisdom. He leaned back, a contemplative expression on his face. "You know, love ain't always easy. There are ups and downs, twists, and turns, but that's what makes it beautiful. It's the willingness to work through the hard times, the sacrifices, the compromises. Love is a journey, not a destination." Adrian nodded, absorbing Jamal's words like a sponge soaking in water. Jamal leaned forward, emphasizing his next words. "Choose love for the right reasons, Adrian. Not for convenience or societal expectations. Choose it because you can't imagine your life without that person. Because they make you a better version of yourself. Treat Amara with kindness, cherish her, and never forget the reasons why you fell in love in the first place. As long as you do that, you will forever have my blessing." Adrian felt a profound gratitude for the advice bestowed upon him by a man who had weathered the storms of life and emerged stronger, guided by the power of love. "Jamal, I hear you loud and clear. Your words mean the world to me, and I want you to know that I'm serious about Amara. I'll do everything in my power to make her happy, to be the partner she deserves." A genuine smile played on Adrian's lips as he continued, "I can't promise it'll always be smooth sailing, but I do promise to destroy any storm that comes our way. Amara is an incredible woman, and I feel blessed to have her in my life." Adrian and Jamal shook hands, the unspoken understanding passing between them, sealed in the firm grip. Just as they released their hold, Amara stepped out, a curious smile playing on her lips. "What are you two chatting about?" she inquired, her eyes moving between her father and Adrian. Adrian chuckled, "Just getting to know each other a bit better. You know, guy stuff." Amara grinned, "I'm sure." She looped her arm through Adrian's, leading him back to the lively gathering. The cookout unfolded into a night of joy and laughter. As the evening unfolded, the love and warmth of Amara's family wrapped around them, creating a sense of belonging that Adrian cherished.

CHAPTER 8

Prince Charming

Adrian arrived at Amara's doorstep, dressed in a sleek black suit that accentuated his confidence. The moment she opened the door, a smile danced on his lips as he admired her beauty. Amara, in a stunning black dress that hugged her curves, greeted him with a teasing grin. "Hey there, handsome," she said, stepping out and linking her arm with his. "Good evening, gorgeous," Adrian replied, leading her toward the sleek black car parked at the curb. As they approached the car, he opened the door for her with. Amara slid into the seat, her eyes locked with Adrian's. The air crackled with anticipation as he closed the door, circling the car to take his place next to her. Amara, gazing at the city lights passing by, couldn't help but feel the magnetic pull between them? Adrian shot her a sideways glance, a smirk playing on his lips. "You know, the So, where are we headed?" Adrian smiled "It's a surprise, you will see once we get there." Amara smiled. She had been seeing Adrian for about 4 months now. She knew he loved taking her on extravagant dates and making her feel special. She had no idea where they were headed but she was sure it would be a night to remember. "Alright, I'm excited to see what you have planned this time. As the city lights painted a vibrant backdrop, their conversation became a dance of words, each exchange revealing more about the depths of their personalities. The car pulled up at the entrance of a tall, sophisticated building that seemed to touch the stars. Adrian walked over to help Amara out of the car. "I never knew this place existed where are we? Adrian leaned in. "Well, it's one of my best-kept secrets. Only special people get invited here," he said with a wink. There was a quiet tension in the air. The click of her heels echoed as they approached the building entrance. Side by side, they walked into the lobby, lit just right to keep things mysterious. Adrian kept the suspense alive. Every step brought more anticipation. They reached the elevators, and as the doors opened, a private lift revealed itself—a ride into a night of magic. As the elevator ascended, a wave of anticipation came over Amara. Adrian, unable to resist the magnetic pull, pressed Amara gently against the mirrored wall. Their eyes locked, a silent agreement passing between them. He traced a slow path with his finger, caressing her arm, then lingering around her lips. His touch sent shivers through Amara, and she leaned into the intimate connection. Adrian's fingers then curled around her neck, pulling her closer. The atmosphere crackled with desire as he sealed the moment with a lingering, passionate kiss, their lips dancing in sync. The elevator doors opened on the top floor, revealing a breathtaking view of the city. They stepped out, the lingering heat of the kiss lingering in the air, and walked into a romantic setting overlooking the twinkling lights below. As they stepped off the elevator, the breathtaking scene unfolded before Amara's eyes. The rooftop was transformed into a haven of romance, with soft fairy lights draped along the edges, casting a warm, golden glow. A table for two, adorned with flickering candles and delicate flowers, stood in the center. The city sprawled beneath them, a mosaic of shimmering lights, and the night sky stretched overhead. The air was filled with a gentle breeze, carrying whispers of the city below. Adrian had created an intimate oasis, a private dinner for just the two of them, overlooking the captivating cityscape. Amara's eyes widened in delight as she took in the thoughtful setup. The ambiance was nothing short of magical, setting the stage for an evening that promised to be filled with shared laughter, meaningful conversations, and the spark of a connection growing stronger with each passing moment. The waiter approached with two exquisite bottles of wine, a rich red and a crisp white. Adrian, with a charming smile, gestured to Amara. "What do you prefer, red or white?" Amara, appreciating the elegance of the moment, chose the red, and the waiter poured a modest amount into their glasses. The glasses clinked, marking the beginning of a night filled with possibilities. As they sipped the wine, the conversation flowed effortlessly. Adrian, leaning back comfortably, fixed his gaze on Amara. "You know, Amara, I've been thinking a lot about what draws me to you. It's not just the physical attraction, although, don't get me wrong, you're stunning. It's something deeper." He continued, his words carrying a sincere warmth. "It's the way your mind works, the depth of your thoughts, the way you see the world. It's the way you speak about your dreams and the passion that radiates from you. That kind of beauty is rare, and I find it incredibly attractive." Adrian leaned in, his eyes fixed on Amara, as he continued to share his thoughts. "It’s more than just attraction; it's admiration. I believe in you and your dreams. The way you talk about your photography, the passion that lights up your eyes when you describe capturing moments – it's infectious. I want to be there beside you as you chase those dreams, supporting you every step of the way." He took a moment, tracing the rim of his wine glass with his fingers, before looking back into her eyes. "You're not just beautiful on the outside, but the strength and determination you carry within are what captivate me. It's rare to find someone who inspires you to be a better version of yourself, and you do that for me. I'm in awe of you, Amara, and I want to be a consistent and positive part of your life, cheering you on as you achieve everything you've set your heart on. Amara, I know it's only been 3 months but, I know that I'm falling in love with you every single day." Amara's gaze dropped momentarily, a shy smile playing on her lips. The soft glow of the city lights outside the window seemed to dance in her eyes as she spoke, each word carrying a weight of genuine emotion. "Adrian, I... I have been so scared to say how I truly feel because I figured I was too early or you just wouldn't feel the same way. But I'm falling in love with you too every single second of the day. You are fine as hell we both know that. But for me it's your whole demeanor, the way you carry yourself with such confidence. I find it so attractive, not just physically, but mentally too. It's easy to talk to you, and when I'm around you. You know I hardly talk about my past; I'm always scared." Her eyes met his, sincerity and vulnerability reflected in them. "When I told you about it, you made me feel safe just by listening. You made me feel like I was releasing such a burden off of me. Being with you feels right, and I can't help but get excited about the possibility of a future together. And I know three months why on earth would I mention a future. But I don't want to miss this or fumble this, I love you Adrian and I hope we build something special." Adrian picked up his glass and clinked it with Amara's. He knew it had not been long but what Amara didn't know is Adrian how purchased an engagement ring after two months. He knew he wanted to marry Amara, but he wanted to be sure she felt the same way first. He had the answer he needed and planned to make the woman in front of him his wife. As the night unfolded, the waiter discreetly delivered a small, elegantly wrapped box to the table. Adrian, a glimmer of excitement in his eyes, slid the box toward Amara. "Open it," he urged, a smile playing on his lips. Amara's fingers delicately untied the ribbon, revealing a dainty long jewelry box. She looked up at Adrian, a mix of curiosity and anticipation in her eyes. Opening the box, she gasped softly at the sight of a beautiful bracelet. Delicate charms adorned it, each one telling a story. "This is for you," Adrian said, his voice warm. "For every memory we make together we will add a charm." Amara examined the charms, her heart swelling with emotion. Among them was a tiny camera, a symbol of their shared memory. She glanced at Adrian, her eyes expressing gratitude and affection. "It's beautiful," she whispered, a genuine smile gracing her face. Adrian took a moment, gazing into Amara's eyes with a warmth that reflected his genuine affection. "I'm glad you like it I want to make memories with you Amara as many as I can." Amara's heart fluttered at the sincerity in his words. The thought of building a collection of charms representing their shared experiences filled her with excitement. "I love you." In the soft glow of the city lights, Adrian leaned across the table, his eyes locked onto Amara's. The air between them crackled with anticipation as he cupped her face with one hand and gently pressed his lips against hers. When Adrian pulled back, a subtle smile played on his lips, “I love you too.” Over the next few months, Amara and Adrian discovered a love that surpassed their wildest dreams. It was a love that unfolded like the petals of a blooming flower. They dined under the stars at cozy rooftop restaurants, the city lights below twinkling like a thousand fireflies. Weekend mornings were reserved staying in and making breakfast together and watching corny movies. Inside jokes that only tickled the both of them. They were creating a bond they never imagined. They began to enter into each other's world and learning more and more about the other. Adrian attended Amara's photography exhibitions, proud to stand by her side as she showcased her art to the world. The glow in her eyes, the radiant smile that graced her lips when she spotted him in the crowd—it was a testament to their shared journey. Conversely, Amara delved into Adrian's world of real estate, attending events where his charisma shined like a beacon. She observed the way he navigated through the social intricacies, leaving an indelible impression with his charm and intellect.

Support became a major foundation of the bases of their relationship. Truly being the other person support allowed them to truly understand who their person was. Who each of them were beyond the mask. They comforted each other through dilemmas they faced. Adrian stood by Amara when doubts about her photography career crept in, reminding her of the brilliance he saw in her art. Amara, in turn, became Adrian's sanctuary, a place where he could take his amour off at the door, and be at peace.

CHAPTER 9

A Dream Come True

"Man, I can't believe we about to make this deal. You know this gone be the biggest one yet. Feel like we could retire out this shit man. Go straight and get out this game. I don't even want to put Amara in none of this. Our entire lives are about to change – it's been one hell of a ride." Adrian's eyes reflected pride and excitement, "Indeed, man we been rocking since we were teenagers. We always wanted to get to this moment. Making plays big enough to retire families." Harrison and Adrian had set up a sale that was going to make them both Adrian millionaires and stay millionaires. Adrian poured himself a drink, the clink of ice cubes echoing the quiet room. "Harrison, remember I told you I was going to a cookout at Amara's people house." Harrison opened a beer "Yea, how was that?" I had a conversation with Amara's father," Adrian continued, his voice tinged with emotion. "I told him I wanted to marry her." Harrison's eyes widened in surprise, "Marriage? Don't you think it's a bit early for all that? I mean you barely even know this girl." Harrison knew his friend was very detached from a lot of people. He never got into relationships, and he never dealt with the same woman for very long. He felt like maybe he was moving too fast.

"Man, I never met someone like Amara before. She's the woman I love, the one I want to spend the rest of my life with." Harrison was happy for his friend but still cautious. The line of work they were in they truly had to be careful of anyone they brought into their lives. "Look man if you are happy, I'm happy for you. All I'm saying is if you gone take this step, you just need to make sure you can trust her. Eventually she will have to know the truth. Can you trust her with that? "Adrian knew Harrison was coming from a place of concern. "I've thought about it long and hard. But I can't let the fear of the unknown dictate my life. I didn't think I would fall in love shit, even you know that. But man I have, and to be honest she makes me want to start looking into going legit. This deal we about to make man, that's putting me right in the place to be able to finally invest into my apartment building. We about to touch a different type of my money my man." Harrison leaned back in his chair, "Out the game? Wait when you start thinking about getting out." Adrian stood up drink in his hand, "Come on Harrison this ain't no new convo man. We been talked about it a while back. We always said we would do this shit until we had enough to get out. Shit we been had enough, more than enough. We forget because we don't flash it but Harrison, we are millionaires. We ain't gotta keep dealing burh." Harrison had a family, and he always knew the time for them to stop dealing would come but he didn't think it would be now. "Listen, I'm all for going fully legit, but man you can't just jump off the porch no plan, nothing, just because you planning to marry Amara. It got to make sense first, that's all I'm saying." Adrian had made up his mind, and nothing and no one could change that. "Of course, I just want to start working that plan now that's all brother. I got you in this life and the next that is no question there." Harrison realized nothing he said would change Adrian's mind so he he got up and poured them both some 1942. "Alright man, well it sounds like congratulations is in order." They held up the glasses to each other "Adrian I've known you for a long time, I have only ever wanted you to be content and happy. You finally found the right woman. Congrats man." They dapped each other up and embraced in a brotherly hug. Harrison looked at his watch and knew he needed to head home. "Aight, man I'm gone head out of here, I need to get to the house." Harrison had his concerns about Adrian's decision to propose but offered support to him, nonetheless. As they parted ways, Harrison whispered to Adrian, "Good luck man. Let me know how it goes." It was Saturday and Adrian couldn't understand the amount of anxiety he was feeling. His palms were shaky, he was so nervous. All he could think of is what if Amara says no. Adrian stepped into the shower. The warm water cascaded over him, washing away the stress of the day. He emerged refreshed, his skin tingling, and wrapped himself in a plush towel. Adrian stood before the mirror, the anticipation building with each moment. He selected a crisp white shirt, tailored black pants. He chose a sleek black suit jacket, the fabric smooth against his skin, and checked his reflection one last time. In that moment, Adrian looked every bit the confident, successful man he had become. His eyes sparkled with determination, and a smile played at the corners of his mouth. Tonight, was the night he would ask Amara to be his forever, and nothing could dim his excitement. On the other side of town, Amara was in full preparation mode for her date night with Adrian. She had her phone on speaker, chatting away with Sasha as she got dolled up. "Girl, I have no idea what that man has planned. He's being all mysterious and shit, lol. I asked him but he just kept saying, it was a surprise." Sasha's voice crackled through the phone, filled with curiosity. "Ooh, spill the tea! What do you think it is?" Amara chuckled, applying a touch of lipstick. "Knowing Adrian, it could be anything. He probably rented out an entire art museum lol you know he goes the super extra mile." Sasha laughed "Girl, that man is always planning something over to the top and special. As

Amara finished getting dressed, a text notification popped up on her phone. "Hold on, let me check this," she said, tapping the screen. "He just texted, the car will be here in 30 min. Bitch, this man got me in a chokehold, you hear me. Damn!" Sasha smiling on the phone "I love this so much for you friend, you deserve it girl, and all I know is he better do right by you. I hate to put him on a t-shirt about you." They both laughed, "Amara, never forget he's the lucky one, ok. And he isn't your ex." Amara smiling at the comment from her friend, "Thank you Sash. "Amara we never talked about those random messages and photo you got again. What happened did they stop?" Amara had forgot about it honestly. She hadn't heard anything else from the mysterious person, so she had really figured it was her ex just trying to be an asshole. "You know what no I never got another note, call or text nothing. I don't know I truly believe it was Marcus. He wanted to get a rise out of me, and when he didn't, he just decided to quit." Sasha chimed in "Or maybe he saw you with Adrian and realized Adrian would kick his ass." They both roared in laughter, "yea you might be right. I don't know but I haven't gotten anything in almost 2 months, so I guess he went back to the hole he crawled out of. Well, let me finish up here and get ready to head out. I will be sure to call you tomorrow and give you all the details. After ending the call with Sasha, Amara did a final check in the mirror, smoothing down her dress and adjusting her hair. She couldn't help but a feel a mix of excitement and nervousness. Adrian always knew how to surprise her, and she was eager to see what he had planned. As she waited for the car to arrive, her mind wandered to all the possibilities. Maybe a romantic dinner at a fancy restaurant? Or maybe a spontaneous get away. Whatever it was she was ready for it. When the car pulled up outside her door, she practically floated down the stairs, her heart flutter with anticipation. The driver greeted her with a smile, and she settled into the backseat, the excitement bubbling inside her. As they drove through the city, Amara couldn't help but imagine what awaited her. She pictured Adrian standing there, a big grin on his face, holding something special just for her. The thought brought a smile to her own face, and she couldn't wait to see him. As Amara stepped out of the car, the soft glow of the garden lights illuminated her figure, casting a radiant aura around her. Adrian couldn't help but be captivated by her beauty. "Wow," he breathed, his eyes tracing her silhouette in the moonlight. "You look absolutely stunning." Amara blushed, feeling a warm flutter in her chest at his words. She wore a sleek black dress that hugged her curves in all the right places, accentuating her elegance and grace. Her hair cascaded down her shoulders her locs beautifully curled and her eyes sparkled with excitement. "Thank you" she said, her voice barely above a whisper. "You look pretty handsome yourself Mr. Bishop." Adrian grinned, offering her his arm as they began to walk through the garden. Amara was speechless as Adrian escorted her into the garden. The pathway was lined with twinkling lights and lanterns, casting a warm glow over everything. The air was filled with the sweet scent of flowers, and the sound of a gentle breeze rustling through the trees. As they walked, towards the garden, Adrian slipped his arm around Amara's waist, drawing her close. "I wanted to create a magical evening that both of us will remember," he said softly, his voice filled with warmth. As they rounded the corner, Amara's eyes widened in surprise. Stretched across the sidewalk were larger-than-life stenciled artworks, each one a photo she had taken with her camera. She stopped in her tracks, her hand flying to her in astonishment. "Oh my God," she gasped, her eyes welling up with tears. "Adrian, is this...?" Adrian smiled, his eyes shining with pride. "It's your art Amara," he said, his voice gentle. "I took some of your favorite photos and had them blown up. Amara was speechless, her heart overflowing with emotion. She walked slowly along the sidewalk, taking in each photo, each memory captured in vibrant detail. She saw the photo of the sunset they had watched together, the picture of the flowers she had photographed in the park on one of their dates, the portrait of her, laughing and carefree that Adrian took of her with her camera. As she reached the end of the sidewalk, she turned to Adrian, her eyes shimmering with tears. “This is the most incredible thing anyone has ever done for me,” she whispered, her voice filled with emotion. “Thank you, Adrian, this is amazing. When did you find the time to do all of this?” “No, worries I have my ways.” Adrian said with a grin on his face. Amara widened her eyes, “Your ways huh. My goodness Adrian thank you so much this is so amazing. Amara went in and kissed Adrian to show her gratitude. “You deserve every bit of it, Amara,” he said softly. “I just wanted tonight to be perfect for you, a night you’ll never forget.” Amara threw her arms around him, holding him tight. She felt overwhelmed with love for this man who had gone above and beyond to make her feel special. As Amara and Adrian walked through the garden, the evening light cast a golden hue over everything, enhancing the beauty of the flowers and foliage around them. The garden was a symphony of colors, with roses of every hue bloomed profusely, their fragrance filling the air. The sound of a sexy saxophone drifted towards them, adding a touch of magic to the already enchanting atmosphere. As they approached the cul-de-sac in the garden Amara was struck by the sight that the cul-de-sac was lined with boxes of long-stemmed roses. The fragrance filled the air, and the soft glow of string lights added a magical touch to the setting. Adrian led her to their table, which was adorned with a stunning bouquet of roses in various hues, casting a warm, romantic ambiance. Amara couldn’t contain her excitement. “Adrian this is absolutely stunning! I can’t believe you did all of this.” Adrian smiled; his eyes filled with admiration. “I wanted tonight to be special.” As they took their seats, a saxophonist began to play softly in the background, adding to the enchanting atmosphere. Amara was captivated by the music, and she looked around in awe at the beauty of the garden. “This is like a dream," she whispered, her voice filled with wonder. As they settled in, the waiter appeared with the first course. Amara's eyes widened in delight as she saw the beautifully presented salmon dish, her favorite. The salmon was perfectly cooked, accompanied by a side of asparagus and a light lemon butter sauce. The aroma was heavenly, and she couldn't wait to dig in. Adrian watched her with a smile, please to see her so happy. "I hope you like it. I wanted tonight to be all about you and what makes you happy." Amara took a bite and closed her eyes, savoring the flavor. "It's amazing," she said, her voice filled with genuine pleasure. "Thank you for this. Adrian. I don't think anyone has ever done something so special for me." As they finished their meal, the saxophonist continued to play, filling the air with soft, melodic tunes. Amara and Adrian laughed and talked, their conversation flowing effortlessly, lost in the magic of the moment. Adrian looked into Amara's eyes, a soft smile playing on his lips. "Amara, would you like to dance?" he asked, holding out his hand. Amara's heart fluttered at his words, and she nodded, placing her hand in his. They stood up, the soft glow of the garden lights illuminating their faces as they moved to the center of the garden. The saxophone played a slow, romantic melody, setting the perfect mood for their dance. Adrian pulled Amara close, his hand resting gently on her waist as they swayed to the music. Amara rested her head on his shoulder, feeling safe and loved in his arms. They danced in what seemed to be silence, lost in each other, the world fading away around the. The night was perfect, the air filled with love and promise. Amara knew in that moment that she had found her soulmate, the one she wanted to spend the rest of her life with. As they danced, Adrian held Amara close, his heart full of love and his mind racing with words he wanted to say to her. He looked into her eyes, seeing the love and trust reflected back to him, and he knew that this was the moment he had been waiting for. He pulled away from Amara and got down on one knee. Amara gasped in surprise as she knew what was about to come. "Amara, you are the most incredible person I have ever known. You have this way of lighting up a room with your smile, of making everyone around you feel loved and cared for. You are kind, compassionate, and endlessly beautiful, both inside and out." Adrian began, his voice soft but filled with conviction. "You've brought so much joy into my life, Amara. You've shown me what it means to truly love someone, to be there for them no matter what. I can't imagine my life without you in int, and I don't ever want to. Adrian continued, his words pouring out from his heart. "As we dance here tonight, surrounded by the beauty of this garden and the music of the saxophone, I can't help but feel like the luckiest man in the world. Amara, will you continue to be my light, my love, and my partner in life, for the rest of my life.?" Amara's eyes filled with tears as she listened to Adrian's words, her heart overflowing with love for him. She nodded, unable to speak, and Adrina's smile grew even wider. He took her hand in his slipping the ring onto her finger and pulled her into a loving embrace. "I promise to always cherish you, to support you, and to love you with all that I am. I can't wait to spend the rest of my life making you happy, Amara. You are my everything," Adrian whispered, his voice filled with emotion. As tears streamed down her cheeks, Amara looked into Adrian's eyes, her heart overflowing with love and emotion. She took a deep breath, trying to compose herself, before speaking. "Adrian, you have no idea how much you mean to me. You are my soulmate. From the moment I met you, I knew I would love you. I knew because I noticed that from day one I started to breath different when I was near you, I walked different next to you, I smile different, I feel different. You drew me to you in a way I had never felt before." Amara began, her voice filled with love and sincerity. "You've shown me what it means to be truly loved, to be cherished and adored. You've supported me, and you've celebrated me. I can't imagine my life without you. Yes, yes, marry you." Adrian gently caressed Amara's cheek, his eyes full of love and tenderness. With a deep, loving gaze, he leaned in capturing her lips in a passionate kiss. Amara melted into his embrace, feeling the warmth of his love enveloping her. The world around the faded away as they shared this intimate moment, lost in each other's presence. The night was still young and the starts twinkled above them, casting a magical glow over the garden. Adrian picked Amara up wrapped her legs around his body and carried her over to a cozy bench nestled under a canopy of blooming flowers. The soft moonlight filtered through the petals, casting a gently glow around them, as if nature itself was setting the stage for their intimate moment. Adrian cupped Amara's face in his hands, his eyes filled with a deep, smoldering desire. He leaned in capturing her lips in a passionate kiss. Amara responded eagerly, her hands roaming over his chest, feeling the heat of his skin beneath her fingertips. Adrian's hands traced the curves of Amara's body, igniting a fire within her that she loved to feel when she was with Adrian. She moaned softly against his lips; lost in the sensation that he evoked in her. Feeling the need for more, Adrian gently lifted Amara, his strong arms supporting her as he carried her to a nearby blanket spread out under the flowers. He laid her down gently, his eyes never leaving hers, filled with a raw passion. Adrian and Amara's embrace deepened; their bodies pressed together in a dance of desire. Adrian's touch ignited a fire within Amara, sending shivers down her spine. She arched into him, craving more of his intensified touch. "I love you" Adrian whispered, his voice husky with desire. "I love you too," Amara replied. Their kisses became more urgent, more desperate, as if trying to convey a lifetime of love and passion in that singular moment. Adrian's hands roamed her body, igniting every nerve ending with touch of heat. Amara's breath hitched as she gave in to the overwhelming sensation that ran through her body, her hands grasping at his back, pulling him closer. "Adrian," she moaned, her voice filled with need. They moved together in a symphony of desire, each touch, each caress a testament to their love and longing for one another. Adrian whispered sweet nothings in her ear, his words a promise of forever. Amara's heart swelled with love, her body responding to his every touch. They made love under the twinkling stars, they sealed their love with a kiss, ready to embark on a new journey together, hand in hand, heart to heart.

CHAPTER 10

Poetic Justice

Amara stepped into the bustling café, the aroma of freshly brewed coffee mingling with the sound of animated conversations. Her heart raced with excitement as she made her way to Sasha's table, eager to share the news that had set her world abuzz. Sasha sat there, a knowing smile on her lips, her eyes bright with curiosity as she watch Amara approach. Amara couldn't contain her excitement as she settled into the seat across from Sasha, her words tumbling out in a rush. "Girl, you won't believe what went down last night! Adrian popped the question! Can you believe it? He asked me to marry him girl." Amara's voice was filled with a mix of exhilaration and disbelief. Sasha's eyes widened in delight, a gasp escaping her lips as she leaned in, eager for every detail. "Oh my goodness Bitch! Shut up!" Sasha hugged Amara and swayed back in fourth out of excitement. "Spill the tea sis. How did it happen? Was it romantic?" Sasha's curiosity was piqued. Amara's laughter filled the café as she regaled Sasha with the tale of Adrian's heartfelt proposal, the tears, the laughter, and the overwhelming rush of emotions. "It was like a scene from a movie Sasha! He took me to this stunning garden, Sasha. It was like a fairytale. I'm walking down the sidewalk and I see photos that I took when me and him were on our dates. You know how I love just taking random photos." Sasha laughed because that was true. "Yes girl you probably got a million of me in that camera." Amara smiled "Exactly, well he took the photos that were memorable to us and blew them up. He had them lined down the entire walk way of the garden. It was like my own mini art gallery. Sasha I couldn't believe it I was so taken back by that type of effort." Amara sipped her drink trying to control the excitement while talking to her best friend. "Then he took me to the this cute little culo-de-sac towards the back of the garden and when we got there it was lined up with long steamed roses all over the place. There were fairy lights, lights on the trees, candles I mean Sasha it was so beautiful. Then out of no where I see someone come around the corner and all I hear is this very soft saxophone being played." Sasha was smiling listening to her friend "Not the Sax, oh honey he was not playing with you last night." They both slapped hands in agreement that Adrian came correct. "Ok, my man did his thing honey. So dinner came out and then he asked me to dance. Girl we were dancing to the sax and then boom he got on one knee and proposed." Amara showed her ring to her friend. "And honey he got a me this big beautiful ass ring, my damn hand heavy." Sasha's eyes gleamed with excitement, her hand reaching out to grasp Amara's in a gesture of shared joy and celebration. "Oh my gosh, Amara that is beautiful. I'm so happy for you!" Amara's eyes sparkled with excitement as she reached into her bag and pulled out a beautifully wrapped gift, a small but meaningful token of their friendship. She handed it to Sasha with a warm smile, anticipation dancing in her eyes. "Sasha, I have something for you, "Amara said, her voice filled with genuine affection. Sasha's eyes widened in surprise as she accepted the gift, a curious expression on her face. She carefully unwrapped it, revealing a card adorned with a collage of pictures of them from childhood until now, a snapshot of their cherished memories. Sasha turned the card over and there was something written on the back. She read it out loud

"In the tapestry of life, you've been my guiding light. Through laughter and tears, you've made everything right. A sister at heart, a friend so true, In every moment I've found solace with you. In the dance of our days, in the whispers of our dreams, You've stood by me, a constant, or so it seems. Through the highs and the lows, the joys and the fears, Your presence, your love has dried up my tears. As I step into a new chapter, a journey of love and grace, I can't imagine it without you, by my side, in this place. Will you stand with me, as my maid of hone, my sister, my friend, together, hand in hand, until the very end? Let's paint the canvas of memories, write the verses of our song, In harmony and laughter, in moments short and long. With you, my dear friend, my sister so dear, every step is lighter, every moment more clear. So here I sand, with a heart full of love and a soul so bright, asking you, my dear friend, to stand with me in this light. Will you be my maid of honor, my sister, so true, we riding together, forever, in all that we do!"

Sasha's eyes welled up with tears as she read the heartfelt poem on the back of the card reminding her of the strong bond she shared with Amara over the years. With a shaky voice and tears rolling down her cheeks, Sasha looked at Amara her best friend, her sister. "Oh, Amara," Sasha's voice couldn't stop cracking and trembling with emotion. "This poem, it takes me back to when we were kids, to the day at lunch when you sat next to me and changed everything. You've always been there for me, through thick and thin. Yes, of course, I'll be your maid of honor. I'll stand by your side, always, just like you've always stood by mine. As Sasha finished her heartfelt response, tears in both her and Amara's eyes, their faces puffy from the emotional moment they had shared. Despite the tears, a sense of lightness and joy filled the air, a testament to the depth of their friendship and the bond that held them together. Amara chuckled through her tears, her voice slightly shaky with emotion. “Look at us, all puffy-faced and shit just looking a mess.” Sasha said jokingly. “At least we are a beautiful mess sister girl” With a playful grin, Sasha added, “Okay, now that we have all that out of the way, let’s go have some celebratory shots. It’s time to toast to this moment.” Amara raised an eyebrow, a hint of hesitation in her expression. “Sasha, it’s not even close to 5o’clock yet. You don’t think it's a bit early for shots.” Sasha waved off her concerns with a mischievous glint in her eye. “Who cares about the time? We’re going to drink to this, baby! Let’s go!” Actually Sasha, let’s go to the liquor store and get a bottle instead. There’s somewhere else I would like to go instead. Sasha with a curious look on her face, shrugged her shoulders and said “Yea sure, where are we going?” Amara placed her money on the table for her tab looked at her friend and said, “I want to go tell my mother the good news.” Sasha knew Amara had issues with her mother, but she also knew not having her mother to talk to or be there for her at such a special moment was probably hard for her. “Ok, let’s go see her.” Amara and Sasha pulled up to her mother’s grave site. A bottle of tequila in hand and two blankets. They approached the grave site and laid their blankets down and took a seat. Amara looked at the headstone she had made for her mother. She didn’t come to her mothers grave that often, but after getting engaged she wanted to talk to her. Sasha could see the hesitation in her friends face. “Amara, go ahead talk to her, I’m right here with you.” As Amara stood before her mother’s grave, the weight of unspoken words and unresolved emotions hung heavy in the air. The memories of a chaotic relationship, full of distance and pain, flooded her mind, intertwining with the knowledge of her mother’s struggles and the layers of her suffering. “Mom,” Amara’s voice quivered, a mix of sorrow and understanding in her words, “I wish I could have understood you better when you were here. The weight of your sadness, your silent battles, they linger in my heart now, clearer than ever before." Tears streamed down Amara's cheeks as she grappled with the truth of her mother's suffering. Knowing about her mother's past trauma now, the pain she endured in silence, opened Amara's eyes to the depth of her mother's struggles. "I get it now, Mom," Amara's voice cracked with emotion, "I understand the tough times you went through, the hurt you kept inside. Your secrets and struggles are now clear to me, a reminder of your strength and pain." A gently breeze whispered through the trees, offering a moment of peace in the cemetery. Amara's words hung in the air, a fragile connection between past regrets and newfound understanding, a tender tribute to a mother who battled her inner demons. "I miss you, Mom," Amara's voice softened, a hint of longing in her words. "I miss the moments we never shared; the words left unspoken. But despite it all, despite the hurt and distance, I love you. I appreciate the fights you faced, the pain you carried, the love you couldn't always express." In that vulnerable moment, Amara found a sense of closure and forgiveness. She made a silent vow to cherish her mother's memory with compassion and empathy, embracing the struggles of their relationship with grace and love, always. "I want you know, Mom," Amara's voice trembled with emotion, "I'm getting married. I've met a man who loves me, who cherishes me. I'm going to be the woman you didn't get the chance to be. I'll carry your love and pain with me, and I'll strive o be the woman you couldn't be. I'll honor your memory in everything I do." Amara turned to Sasha with tear stained cheeks and bittersweet smile. The weight of the emotions that had surfaced during their visit. "Sasha," Amara's voice was soft, tinged with a mix of sadness and gratitude, "Thank you for being here with me today. It means the world to me." Sasha, her eyes filled with tears, curiosity and concern, looked at Amara with a gentle expression. "Girl you know I will always be here for you. But what did you mean earlier, about understanding your mothers past now?" Amara paused for a moment, her gaze drifting back to her mother's resting place, before turning back to Sasha with a wistful smile. "I just understand her more now that she's gone. Now that I'm older, I know that she struggled and carried a lot of pain. She could only love me the best way she knew how. I just really understand her now, that's all." Sasha, still not sure exactly what Amara meant she nodded in understanding. "Okay, I get. Let's head out, Amara. Are you ready?" Amara nodded, a sense of peace settling within her as she took one last glance at her mother's grave, a silent farewell. They left the cemetery, their hearts heavy with memories but filled with a newfound sense of understanding. As Amara and Adrian sat down to discuss the wedding details, the air was filled with a mix of excitement and anticipation. They had already gone through the list of potential venues and color schemes, but the topic of the guest list loomed before them, a reminder of the complexities that often come with panning a wedding. Amara watched Adrian, a soft smile playing on her lips as she admired the way his eyes list up when he talked about their future together. She knew that beneath his confident exterior, there were layers of emotions and memories that shaped his perspective on family and relationships. "Adrian," Amara began, her voice gentle and warm, "I was thinking about the guest list for the wedding. It's such an important part of the day, and I want to make sure we're both comfortable with who we invite." Adrian nodded, his gaze meeting hers with a mixture of curiosity and apprehension. He knew that the topic of family could be a sensitive one, especially when it came to his own history. "I know that your relationship with your mother is complicated," Amara continued, her words carefully chosen. "I can't imagine how difficult it must be for you, not having her in your life. But I wanted to talk to you about that possibility of inviting her to the wedding. It's a big decision, and I want to support you in whatever you feel is best." Adrian's expression softened, a flicker of vulnerability crossing his features. The wounds of his past were still raw, the absence of his mother a void that had shaped his journey in ways he couldn't fully articulate. "She left when I was just a kid," Adrian spoke, his voice tinged with a mix of sadness and resignation. "I haven't seen or spoken to her in years. I don't see any reason she would need to be present on our wedding day. She gave birth to me, but that's it. I'm good baby." Amara reached out to take Adrian's hand a gesture of comfort and solidarity. "I understand, Adrian. This decision is yours to make, and I'll support you no matter what you want to do." As the conversation about the wedding planning turned playful, Amara and Adrian found themselves joking and teasing each other about the small details. They debated over cake flavors, dance songs. Amara couldn't help but laugh at Adrian's exaggerated dance moves as he tried to demonstrate their potential first dance. "Oh, damn I had no idea my man couldn't dance. Baby boy gone need some dance lessons before we walk down that aisle!" she teased, a smile tugging in the corners of her lips. Adrian flashed her a grin, his eyes lighting up with mischief. "Hey, I'll have you know I've got some killer dance moves up my sleeve. Baby you just wait and see!" Amara and Adrian laughed. "Are you sure you want to do this so quick. I mean I understand the venue only had one cancellation this year but it is literally only 34 days away. Do you think we will have everything done and ready by then?" Adrian put down the guest list and looked at Amara. "Listen here little lady. You said that venue was your dream place to get married. They are booked for the next 2 years and somehow, they had a cancellation the same day you called. That means we are meant to have our wedding there, so that is what you will have. 34 or 4 days, baby I could marry you tomorrow." Amara smiled she knew she had hit the jackpot with Adrian, and she couldn't wait to marry this man. They kissed softly to signify their love. Amara looked at her watch, "Woah mister, before you get started, I have to go meet my stepmother and dad for lunch." They kissed each other goodbye. Amara was leaving the apartment and she looked back at Adrian and said, "I can't wait to Mrs. Bishop, you have no idea." As Amara her dad, and stepmom sat down for lunch at a nice steakhouse, the atmosphere was filled with comforting sounds of clinking cutlery and the sizzling of steaks on the grill. Amara's dad, a hint of concern in his voice "Hey baby girl, I'm glad we sitting here. Now I looked at that place you said you having the wedding. And maybe I was a little sleepy but I know damn well I didn't see that the venue alone cost 25,000. Because I 'm trying to figure out who the hell gone pay that shit." Amara and Evelyn burst out in laughter at her dads remark. "Yall laughing, I'm serious. Do that come with anything. I'm assuming it come with the bar, the workers, the video, the damn wedding dress everything. It got to be all inclusive for a ticket of 25,000!" Amara tapped her dad on the shoulder, "Dad, I did not call you here to talk about paying for the wedding. Adrian is pretty successful, he will cover all of the wedding cost." Amara's father nodded his head in understanding, "Now see that is a son in law I like to have. Yes mam, now that we know I ain't got to pay for no wedding, I'll cover lunch." Evelyn laughed at her husband, "You so silly, baby girl I know you said you wanted to have lunch because there were some things you wanted to discuss with us. Everything alright?" Amara smiled "Yea, ma everything is perfect. I wanted to meet with the both of you to kind of tell you some of the plans for before and on my wedding day." Amara turned to her dad "Dad you have truly been my rock for so long. With everything that I have been through you have always been there for me. Daddy's little girl, always protecting me." Amara's dad grabbed her hand, "I will always protect you baby girl. I know I didn't protect you in your past relationship because I didn't know but that will never ever happen again. I got you." Amara knew her father didn't know about her abusive relationship, and she never held that against him. "I know daddy, it's ok. I'm happy now, I finally got the man I've always wanted. Will you walk me down the aisle and give me away on my wedding day?" "Of course, baby girl, you would have had anybody else doing it, I was gone pop 'em on sight." They all laughed "Daddy!" Amara said as she pushed his arm in a joking way. She turned to her stepmom, "Ma, as you know my mother is not here to share this moment with me at all. But I am blessed to have a second mother who loves me as if she birthed me. Would you join me and Sasha while I pick out my wedding gown, and also help me get ready on the day of my wedding?" Evelyn didn't have children of her own, she helped raise Amara after her mother died. She was overwhelmed with emotion to hear Amara ask her to step up for her on her special day. With tears in her eyes, she responded to Amara "Of course Amara. I will help with anything you need. I am so excited for you Amara and so happy for you and Adrian. I can tell he truly makes you happy, and you being happy makes me so happy for you." Amara knew her stepmother truly cared for her and stepped up in a major way with her when she lost her mother. She was forever grateful to have her in her life. The waiter approached the table and touched Amara on her shoulder and asked her "Is your name Amara?" Amara looked at her with a confused look on her face not sure why she was asking or how she would know her real name. "Yes my name is Amara." The waiter handed her an envelope that was blank on the front. Her parents were looking at her curiously "What is it?" Amara not sure what it was "I'm not sure maybe it's a gift from the restaurant, or something I don't know" Amara opened the envelope and there was a card on the front that said congratulations you're getting married. She opened the card and it read "Congratulations on your engagement! Wishing you a lifetime of love, happiness, and beautiful memories together as you embark on this wonderful journey of marriage. Cheers to the happy couple!" At the bottom of the card it said 'Amara, remember that shadows can't hide the truth forever. The mask will slip, revealing what lies beneath. Watch your back, for secrets have a way of finding their way into the light.' Signed with 'You Know.' Upon reading the mysterious message, Amara's heart raced with a mix of fear and recognition. The unsettling words hinted at a past she had tried to bury, and she knew that someone from her history held the key to her secrets. Determined to confront the truth and put an end to the looming threat, Amara felt a sense of urgency to meet with this person and unravel the mysteries of her past. The realization dawned on her, she had to address the problem, before it became a real problem. As Amara sat at the table with her parents, she casually mentioned that the card was from someone in the restaurant who had recognized her and wanted to congratulate her on her upcoming wedding. She assured her parents that everything was fine and that she had to run errands later in the day. With a smile, she said goodbye to her parents and excused herself from the table, eager to address the person who has been trying to invade her life over the past few months. Amara walked out of the restaurant and pulled out her cellphone. She knew she couldn't tell anyone what she was about to do but she knew she had to do it before everything was ruined. She sent a text to someone that said, 'meet me on the hill.' Amara's car came around and she got in it and drove towards the meeting spot. She pulled up to a older looking house that sat up on a slight hill. The house looked to be abandoned and you could tell no one actually lived there. Amara got out of the car and walked up the hill into the house. As she approached the house there was a music playing on the inside. She could hear music playing from the inside of the house. She could feel her anxiety was high and she knew she shouldn't be there, but she knew she needed to be. She opened the door and there he sat. Marcus Amara's ex-boyfriend. He was sitting on the couch looking at through an old photo album of them together. He looked up at her and smiled a mysterious smile on her face. "Well hello wife, how have you been?" Amara took a deep breath and walked into the house. "So, it has been you, watching and following me. Sending me these stupid ass notes. Why?" Marcus sat back and looked at Amara, "You look good Amara. I mean I guess I would look good too if I was about to get married to some rich ass man, and knowing I'm still married to my ex." Amara squinted her eyes and looked at Marcus "I only married you because I needed someone. I was lost and you came along. Then you started beating on me and I wanted out." Marcus laughed, "Beating on you? Yea, that's right, that is the story you started to tell everyone isn't it?" Amara with confusion on her face "Telling everyone? Oh so now the abuse didn't happen? You never hit me? You still sticking with that crock of shit huh?" Marcus tilted his head to the said looking at Amara, "Ok, well since I was such a horrible person, someone you hate so much, why won't you divorce me Amara? I mean you can't get married, and you're still legally married to me. Or does no one still know that?" Amara turned around and looked at Marcus "You want me to divorce you so you can take half of my money. But you don't deserve a dime of it, you were abusive, manipulative, and a liar the entire time we were together. I tried to get away from you and you did everything in your power to find me every time. I have paid you like clock rock every month 5000 I haven't missed a payment. Why are you here?" Marcus smiled and walked into the kitchen; Amara followed him. "I came into some more recent opportunities and I need 25,000 to take advantage of it. Oh yea and seeing that you're getting married now to Mr. Big Money those 5,000 dollar payments, needs to increase to 10,000 monthly. Amara upset yelled "Are you fucking kidding me! I can't do either of those things. I can't give you 25,000 and I can't increase it to 5,000 a month. Have you lost your mind?" Marcus laughed out loud "Naw, I haven't but you about to, if you don't get me that money. See Amara what you forget is I know who you, the real you. Your dad, your stepmom, Sasha, Adrian, nobody knows who Amara really is do they? Nobody except me. I know what you are really capable of, I know you better than you know yourself. Which is why I know you will make a way to get me exactly what it is I am asking for. Because make no mistake if you don't, I will tell everything I know." Amara put her head on the table, she knew Marcus would blow up everything if she didn't get him the money. "Ok, ok, listen I need a few days to get the money together. I don't have 25,000 just sitting in my bank account." Marcus didn't care about Amar's excuses he needed the money and expected her to get it for him. "I really don't care how you get the money Amara all I know is that you better get it. I'm in town for a few weeks, but I need the money by this Sunday before I lose my moment. I will be here Sunday at 11am and I expect you to show up with the money. Because if you don't," he leaned over and whispered in Amara's ear "I know so much more than you think, and not even Jesus himself will be able to save you from this shit." Marcus stroked Amara's hair kissed her on top of her head and said, "I'll see you Sunday, honey." Marcus turned around and walked out the back door to leave. Amara sat in the kitchen of this old, abandoned house. It was the house her and Marcus has rented out together. The owner denied when they lived there, and he left the house to the both of them. They never sold the home and neither of them lived there. Amara couldn't believe what had just happened. Marcus was going to ruin everything if she didn't find a way to get him the money. She checked all of her accounts and in total she had 29,543 dollars. She knew giving him that money would literally deplete her back account but at this point she didn't have a choice. She wasn't sure where the 10,000 would come from the next month but she figured she would be ok because she had some really important gigs coming up soon. Push come to shove she could just tell Adrian she wants to move in with him sooner and let her apartment go sooner before the wedding. All she did know was if she didn't get Marcus the 25,000 by Sunday, he would destroy everything she had put into motion. She got up and grabbed her things and left the house. It was after 5 so she couldn't go to the bank. Tomorrow was Thursday and she had to work all day long and she knew her, and Adrian had planned all weekend. How would she get away from him to go to the bank and make sure a large withdrawal. Amara had to come up with a plan that would allow her to do what she had to do. Time was ticking and she had to make sure she got Marcus out of her life before he tried to tell Adrian too much and destroy her life. Amara knew what she had to do. If she gave Marcus, the money he would just keep coming back for more. Marcus had to disappear permanently. Amara went in her trunk and opened the area where she kept her spare tire. She took out a phone in a plastic bag and powered it on. She sent a text to an unknown number 'I have a job, rate still the same?' The person on the other end responded '15.' This was the only option she had to remove Marcus from the picture. She replied to the text 'tomorrow meet me by the swing 8.' Amara powered the phone off, put it back in the trunk, got in her car and drove off.

CHAPTER 11

Breathe of Fresh Air

It was Friday and she had some many wedding plans to finish up. She was meeting her mother and Sasha today to try on dresses and hopefully find her fit. She knew she had to be done with them by 7:00 so she could do what she needed to do. But she didn't want them to sense that anything was off so she made sure to play it cool. She had told them to meet her at the store around 12:00, they were going to shop for dresses and then go for lunch. Sasha and Evelyn were already there waiting for Amara to arrive. They were well into their 2nd glass of champagne, her step mom was a lightweight so she was already feeling good. "Amara, darling, we've been waiting for! You're just in time to start trying on some gorgeous gowns," Evelyn exclaimed. Amara saw the drink in her step moms hand and knew she was in for some fun banter. "Hi ma, I see you've started already." Amara hugged Sasha, "Hey best friend! I am so glad you're here" Amara smiled, grateful for the opportunity to focus on something other than her worries. She joined them at the racks of beautiful dresses, each one more stunning than the last. As she browsed through the selection, she couldn't help but feel a sense of joy and excitement for her upcoming wedding. Evelyn, always the fashionista, eagerly picked out a few dresses for Amara to try on. “Oh, this one would look stunning on you, dear. And this one, oh my it’s simply divine!” she gushed, her eyes full of excitement. Amara grabbed both dress her step mom had showed her “I think these are beautiful too, let me try to them on.” Amara went to the back to get changed. As Amara tried on dress after dress, each one more stunning than the last, she couldn't shake the feeling that something was missing. The gowns were beautiful, elegant, and perfectly tailored, but none of them seemed to capture the essence of who she was and what she wanted to convey on her wedding day. Sasha and Evelyn oohed and aahed at each dress, their eyes wide with admiration. "Oh, Amara, you look absolutely breathtaking in that one!" Sasha exclaimed, while Evelyn nodded in agreement, her face beaming with pride. But despite their enthusiasm, Amara couldn't ignore the nagging feeling that none of the dresses had the "it factor" she was looking for. She longed for a gown that would make her feel truly radiant and confident on her special day. As she stepped out in the eleventh dress, a vision of lace and silk that shimmered in the soft light of the fitting room, Amara couldn't help but feel a twinge of disappointment. The dress was undeniably beautiful, but it still didn't quite feel like "the one." Sasha and Evelyn exchanged concerned glances, sensing Amara's hesitation. "Is everything alright, darling?" Sasha asked, her voice filled with genuine concern. Amara took a deep breath, her mind racing with thoughts of Marcus and the looming deadline. Despite her inner turmoil, she forced a smile and replied, "I just... I don't know. None of these dresses feel quite right. I want something that makes me feel truly myself, you know?" Sasha and Evelyn shared a knowing look, understanding the depth of Amara's desire to find the perfect gown. "Don't worry, dear. We'll keep looking until we find that one special dress that speaks to your heart," Evelyn reassured her, her voice filled with warmth and understanding. As Amara stood in the fitting room, feeling a sense of uncertainty about the dresses she had tried on so far, a store worker approached her with a knowing look in her eyes. "Excuse me, Miss, I couldn't help but overhear your conversation. I think I may have just the dress you're looking for," the store worker said, her tone filled with confidence. Amara looked up, intrigued by the store worker's words. "Really? What dress is it?" she asked, a spark of hope igniting in her eyes. The store worker smiled warmly and replied, "It's a custom design from one of our newer designers. We just received it yesterday, and I have a feeling it may be exactly what you're searching for. The dress is called 'Lizzy.'" Amara's heart skipped a beat at the mention of the dress's name. "Lizzy? That's... that was my mother's name," she whispered, her voice filled with emotion. The store worker nodded; her eyes filled with understanding. "I thought your mother's name was Evelyn." Amara paused, a hint of sadness flickering in her eyes. "No, Evelyn is my stepmother. I lost my biological mom when I was young. Her name was Elizabeth, but everyone called her Lizzy," she explained, her voice tinged with emotion. Wow, what a beautiful coincidence, isn't it? The dress is as unique and special as its namesake. Would you like to try it on? I have a feeling it may be the one you've been looking for," she said, her voice gentle and reassuring. Amara's hands trembled slightly as she nodded, her heart filled with a mix of anticipation and trepidation. Could this dress named after her beloved mother truly be the one that would make her feel like the radiant bride she longed to be? With a sense of reverence, the store worker led Amara to the back of the store, where the dress called "Lizzy" awaited her. As she stepped into the gown, she felt a rush of emotions wash over her, a sense of connection and love that transcended time and space. And as she looked at herself in the mirror, dressed in the exquisite gown that bore her mother's name, Amara knew in her heart that she had finally found the dress that captured the essence of who she was and the legacy of love that her mother had left behind. In that moment, surrounded by the support and love of her family, Amara felt a sense of peace and joy that she knew would carry her through the challenges and triumphs that lay ahead. As Amara took a deep breath and prepared to step out of the fitting room in the dress named "Izzy," a sense of anticipation and emotion filled the air. The store worker, aware of the significance of the moment, announced softly, "She's coming out now in the dress known as 'Izzy.'" As the fitting room door opened, Amara emerged, a vision of beauty and grace that took everyone's breath away. The gown named after her late mother, Elizabeth, enveloped her in a cascade of delicate lace and flowing silk, creating a stunning silhouette that seemed to glow with a radiant light. The bodice of the dress was adorned with intricate floral lace appliques that shimmered in the soft light of the store, creating a sense of ethereal beauty and timeless elegance. The sweetheart neckline accentuated Amara's collarbones and shoulders, adding a touch of romance to the overall design. As she walked towards her stepmother, Evelyn, and her best friend, Sasha, who were both seated in awe, they couldn't help but stand up in reverence at the sight of Amara in the exquisite gown. Tears glistened in their eyes as they took in the beauty and significance of the moment. The fitted waistline cinched in Amara's figure, accentuating her curves, and creating a flattering silhouette that exuded confidence and grace. The skirt flowed gracefully to the floor, cascading into a sweeping train that trailed behind her with every step, creating a sense of grandeur and majesty. The back of the dress was a work of art, featuring a dramatic low-cut design that showcased Amara's back in an elegant and alluring way. The lace appliques continued down the back of the gown, creating a stunning visual effect that captivated everyone in the room. As Amara reached Evelyn and Sasha, they both reached out to her, their eyes filled with tears of joy and love. In that moment, surrounded by the support and admiration of her loved ones, Amara felt a deep sense of connection to her mother's memory and a profound gratitude for the journey that had led her to this poignant and unforgettable moment. The dress named "Izzy" had not only captured the essence of who Amara was and the legacy of love her mother had left behind but had also transformed her into a vision of beauty and strength that would carry her through the challenges and triumphs of the days to come. As Amara stood before Evelyn and Sasha in the gown named "Izzy," a moment of profound emotion and connection filled the room. Sasha, understanding the significance of the dress's name, whispered softly, "Lizzy," a single word that held a world of meaning for Amara. Tears welled up in Amara's eyes as she looked at Sasha, feeling the weight of her mother's memory and the love that surrounded her in that moment. Evelyn, moved by the depth of emotion in the room, reached out and took Amara's hand, a silent gesture of support and love. "Now you can have her walking down the aisle with you," Evelyn said, her voice filled with warmth and tenderness. Without hesitation, she and Sasha walked over to the stage, standing beside Amara as they looked at their reflections in the mirror. Amara felt a rush of gratitude and love as she stood with her stepmother and best friend, their tears mingling with hers as they shared in the beauty and significance of the moment. The three women stood together, hand in hand, a bond of love and support that transcended words. As they gazed at their reflections in the mirror, tears streaming down their faces, Amara whispered, "This is the dress." In that moment, surrounded by the love and understanding of Evelyn and Sasha, Amara knew that she had found not just a gown but a symbol of love, connection, and the enduring power of family. The dress named "Izzy" was more than just fabric and lace; it was a testament to the strength and resilience that had carried Amara through the challenges of her past and the promise of a bright and beautiful future ahead. And as she stood with her loved ones by her side, Amara felt a sense of peace and joy that she knew would carry her through the moments of joy and celebration that awaited her on her wedding day. As the emotional moment in the wedding dress store came to a close, Amara wiped away her tears and prepared to pay for the gown named "Izzy." The store worker smiled warmly, sensing the significance of the moment, as Amara settled the payment with a grateful heart. After leaving the store, Amara, Evelyn, and Sasha made their way to a charming bistro around the corner, where they settled into a cozy table and began discussing the last-minute details of the upcoming wedding. With only 33 days left until the big day, they knew they had to ensure everything was perfect for the intimate celebration with their closest loved ones. As they sipped on their drinks and shared stories and laughter, the conversation turned to the wedding decorations, the dresses, and the overall vision for the special day. Amara shared her idea of having both Evelyn and Sasha wear white, along with all the guests, creating a cohesive and elegant theme for the celebration. "I want both of you in white, looking as stunning as ever," Amara said, her eyes shining with excitement. "I'll be covering the cost of your dresses, so feel free to choose any style that makes you feel beautiful and special on the day." Evelyn and Sasha were touched by Amara's generosity and thoughtfulness, expressing their gratitude for being a part of such a meaningful occasion. They eagerly discussed their dress options, each envisioning themselves in a gown that reflected their individual style and personality. As the conversation turned to the honeymoon, Evelyn and Sasha couldn't help but ask about Amara's plans. With a smile, Amara explained that she and Adrian were postponing their honeymoon to Jamaica due to some work-related commitments Adrian had to attend to first. "We'll be heading to Jamaica for our honeymoon once Adrian takes care of his meetings," Amara shared, a sense of anticipation and excitement evident in her voice. "I can't wait to relax and celebrate our love in paradise after all the wedding festivities are over." As they chatted at the bistro, Sasha noticed that Amara seemed a bit different, like she had something on her mind.

Sasha leaned in and asked gently, "Hey, Amara, everything okay? You seem a little distracted today." Amara put on a smile and said, "Oh, I'm fine, just feeling a bit tired with work and all the wedding stuff. Just need some rest, that's all." Even though Amara tried to brush it off, Sasha could tell something was bothering her. She knew Amara well and could see that she was holding something back, even if she didn't want to admit it. Unbeknownst to Evelyn and Sasha, Amara was carrying a heavy load of worries about Marcus and the secrets she had to keep hidden. She couldn't tell them about her past with Marcus, the threats he made, or the fear that was eating away at her. They didn't know about the tough times Amara had been through with Marcus or the things she had to keep buried deep down. Amara knew she had to keep this to herself, shielding her loved ones from the dark parts of her past. As they continued chatting about the wedding plans, Amara tried to push aside her inner struggles and focus on the happiness of the upcoming celebration. She knew the road to her wedding day wouldn't be easy, but she also believed she had the strength to face whatever challenges came her way, even if she had to deal with them alone. As Amara sat at the bistro with Evelyn and Sasha, enjoying their time together and celebrating the wedding plans, her phone rang with Adrian's call. She answered with a smile, the chatter and laughter of the bistro providing a lively backdrop to their conversation. "Hey, Adrian, what's up?" Amara said, a hint of playfulness in her voice. Adrian's voice came through the phone, warm and reassuring. "Hey, babe, just wanted to let you know I need to catch up with Harrison about some things. I'll swing by your place later tonight, around 9 or 10." Amara chuckled, the joy of the moment mingling with the relief of Adrian's call. "Sounds good, Adrian. I guess I'll have to get Evelyn and Sasha an Uber home at this rate," she joked, a twinkle in her eye as she glanced at her companions. Evelyn and Sasha joined in the laughter, the mood light and carefree as they continued to enjoy their time together. The bistro buzzed with energy and warmth, a perfect backdrop for their celebration and camaraderie. As Amara said her goodbyes to Evelyn and Sasha outside the bistro, she hugged them tightly, feeling grateful for their friendship and support. "Thank you both for tonight. I'll see you soon," Amara said, a smile on her face. Evelyn returned the embrace, her eyes filled with warmth. "Take care, dear. We'll talk soon," she said, her voice filled with love and concern. Sasha chimed in, "You've got this, Amara. We're always here for you," her words a reassuring reminder of their unwavering friendship. With a final wave, Amara headed towards the valet stand to retrieve her car. As she waited, she felt a mix of emotions swirling inside her. The cool evening air brushed against her skin, carrying a sense of anticipation and nerves as she prepared to meet the mysterious recipient of her anonymous text. Finally, her car pulled up, and she climbed in, the engine purring to life as she navigated the streets towards the park. The familiar route felt different tonight, charged with a sense of intrigue and uncertainty that kept her on edge. As she parked near the entrance of the park, Amara took a deep breath, steeling herself for the meeting that awaited her. The park was quiet and dimly lit, casting shadows that danced in the moonlight, adding to the air of mystery that surrounded her clandestine rendezvous. With a determined heart and a steady resolve, Amara stepped out of her car and made her way towards the designated meeting spot, her mind racing with questions and possibilities. As Amara approached the swings in the dimly lit park, her heart pounded with a mix of fear and determination. The shadows seemed to dance around her, casting an eerie glow on the scene unfolding before her. Suddenly, a figure emerged from the darkness, wearing a black ski mask that concealed their identity mostly. The only thing you could really every see what a scare that went over his left eye lid, it was as if someone had cut him before.. The mysterious person stood silently, a looming presence that sent shivers down Amara's spine. Without a word spoken, Amara handed the envelope containing $15,000 and a photo of the person to the masked figure. Alongside the items was a slip of paper detailing a date, time, and location. The figure took the envelope and, without hesitation, pulled out a lighter and set everything ablaze. As the flames consumed the evidence before her eyes, Amara felt a surge of conflicting emotions wash over her. A sense of relief mingled with guilt and apprehension, knowing that she had just set in motion a plan to rid herself of Marcus, the looming threat that had cast a shadow over her life. Once the flames died down and the mysterious figure turned away, disappearing into the darkness, Amara stood alone in the park, the weight of her actions settling heavily on her shoulders. She knew that what she had done was necessary to protect herself and her future with Adrian, but the gravity of her decision weighed heavily on her conscience. As she stood in the quiet stillness of the park, the reality of the situation sank in. Amara knew that she had taken a drastic step to ensure her safety and happiness, but the consequences of her actions loomed large in the shadows of the night. With a heavy heart and a resolute spirit, she turned and made her way back to her car, the echoes of her choices reverberating in the silence of the night. She pulled out her phone and sent a text to Marcus 'I got it, meet me on the hill at 12.' Marcus replied right away 'Good girl.' As Amara made her way back to her car, the weight of her actions lingering in the silence of the night, on the other side of town, Adrian sat with Harrison in a dimly lit bar, the gravity of their conversation hanging heavy in the air. The contrast between Amara's clandestine meeting in the park and Adrian's discussion with Harrison about their future plans underscored the diverging paths their lives were taking. Adrian took a sip of his drink, the clink of ice against glass breaking the silence between them. "You know, Harrison, it's time for us to make a change," Adrian said, his voice tinged with a mix of determination and uncertainty. Harrison raised an eyebrow, a look of surprise crossing his face. "A change?

What are you talking about, man?" he asked, a hint of curiosity in his tone. Adrian leaned in, his gaze focused and intense. "After our last deal, I've made up my mind. I'm getting out of this sh*t," he said, a note of finality in his voice. Harrison's eyes widened, a mix of shock and concern in his expression. "Damn, Adrian, are you serious? What about the business, the money?" he asked, a touch of apprehension creeping into his words. Adrian nodded, a sense of resolve in his demeanor. "I want you to take over, Harrison. You're my boy, and I know you can handle this shit," he said, a hint of pride in his voice. Harrison let out a low whistle, a mix of surprise and respect in his reaction. "Well, shit, Adrian, if you're out, I'm out too. We got in this game when we was kids because we had too. The only reason I still been rocking is because of the pact we made. I been ready to retire out this shit, hell my old lady been ready for me to do that too. We got so much money out here invested, shit the residual we been getting is more than enough. So you out I'm out. Who else can you get to run this shit?" They both laughed, Adrian hopped his friend would get out with him. So he had a backup plan. He had a business man in Atlanta one of his most trusted soldiers. He had been dedicated to Harrison and Adrian for many years. He knew he was young and still eating. "Man, I was hoping you said that, so cool. I think Mayo would be second runner up. He's smart, doesn't make dumb decisions, he not flashy, he just be in his own lane. I think giving this empire over to him would be smart." Harrison nodded in agreement. They had both help bring Mayo in the game. He took care of his siblings because his parents were usually high or in jail. He didn't make dumb decisions. Harrison trusted Adrian's decision. "I agree Mayo would be perfect. On this last deal we make let's let them know we gone bring Mayo and we can make the hand off then. Then we done with this shit." They held their glasses up and Adrian made a toast "To getting out". Harrison held up his drink and repeated "To getting out." The two friends continued to talk late into the night, their conversation peppered with colorful language and shared memories of their time in the game. As they discussed their plans for the future, the weight of their decisions hung heavy in the air, but the bond of friendship and camaraderie between them remained unbreakable. As the conversation between Adrian and Harrison came to a close, Adrian checked the time and realized he had to head home. "Man, I gotta go. My fiancée is probably waiting for me," Adrian said with a chuckle, prompting Harrison to join in the laughter. They shared a few jokes and banter before Adrian reminded Harrison about their appointment to get fitted for their tuxedos the next day. "Don't forget, we've got that tux appointment tomorrow. I'll see you in the morning, man," Adrian said, giving Harrison a friendly dap before they went their separate ways. Adrian hopped into his car and drove home, the anticipation of seeing Amara building with each passing mile. As Adrian pulled into the driveway, and entered in Amara's place. There were boxes everywhere from her packing up. After the wedding Amara was moving in with Adrian and moving out of her place. As he walked towards the bedroom, he heard the shower running. He walked in and followed the sound to the bathroom. The steam from the hot water filled the room as he opened the door and saw Amara in the shower. The warm, comforting air surrounded him as he called out to her, "Hey, babe, I'm home." Adrian watched her in the shower, feeling grateful for the love they shared and looking forward to their future together. Amara turned around and smiled at him "Well hello Mr. Bishop I'm so glad you're home. Get in." Adrian smiled eager to follow orders. He took off his clothes and joined Amara in the shower. He met her with a beautiful, shared kiss that signified how happy he was to come to her. They made love in the shower. Adrian had finally found what he felt he had missed this entire time and he couldn't be happier. As they woke up on a beautiful Sunday morning, Amara and Adrian continued the task of packing up Amara's house. Amara was moving in with Adrian in just a few weeks, she had so much left to do. Amara hummed a soft tune in the kitchen, the comforting scents of breakfast wafting through the air as she prepared a meal to fuel their day. Meanwhile, Adrian was in the living room, surrounded by boxes filled with memories and mementos of Amara's past. As Adrian sifted through the boxes, his hands came across a stack of old newspapers, their yellowed pages holding stories of the past. Curiosity piqued, he began to search through the articles, his eyes scanning the headlines that spoke of a dark chapter in the University of Georgia's history. The intense words detailing the series of rapes that had shaken the community sent a chill down his spine, the reality of the crimes hitting close to home. With a heavy heart, Adrian read through the articles, each word painting a vivid picture of the pain and trauma endured by the victims. The faces of the women, their stories of survival and strength, left a deep impact on him, the weight of their suffering printed right on the pages before him. As he came across the article detailing the arrest of his own father and the heinous crimes he had committed, a wave of shock and disbelief washed over him, the revelation striking at the core of his being. One particular detail in the articles made Adrian cringe, a chilling description that cut through him like a knife, leaving a profound sense of unease in its wake. The realization of the horrors that had unfolded, the lives shattered, and the scars left behind, left him reeling with a mix of emotions. His father was the cause of so many women's pain, but he had never known just how far his father had went. Feeling a surge of confusion and turmoil, Adrian made his way to the kitchen where Amara was cooking, his heart heavy with the weight of the reminder of what pain his father had caused. With a deep breath, he approached her, his voice filled with a mixture of concern and apprehension. "Amara, what's going on? Why are you digging into my father's past?" he asked, the words hanging in the air, a reflection of the tumultuous thoughts swirling within him. "I was honest with you about him, am I missing something?" As Adrian's gaze bore into Amara with a mixture of confusion and concern, she felt a wave of uncertainty wash over her. The weight of the situation pressed down on her as she struggled to find the right words to explain the stack of newspapers he had stumbled upon. Her mind raced with a tumult of emotions, her past trauma and fears bubbling to the surface. With a furrowed brow and a troubled expression, Amara took a deep breath and began to speak, her voice tinged with a hint of vulnerability. "Adrian, I... I got those newspapers when you first told me about your father," she started, her words hesitant and filled with unease. "I... I wanted to read the stories of the victims, to try to understand and make sure... to make sure you weren't like him." Adrian's eyes widened in surprise, a mix of emotions flickering across his face. He reached out a hand towards Amara, a gesture of reassurance and understanding. "Amara, I had no idea you were feeling this way. You don't have to be afraid, I'm not like him," he said, his voice filled with sincerity and a touch of sadness. Amara's gaze met Adrian's, a glimmer of hope and fear mingling in her eyes. "I know, Adrian, I trust you. It's just... with everything that happened in the past, I couldn't help but worry," she confessed, her voice soft and filled with emotion. Adrian nodded, his expression one of empathy and compassion. "I get. But baby, I wish you would have told me. I'm here for you, and I'll always be honest with you," he reassured her, his words a promise of trust and support. "You are the most important thing to me. But you got to tell me when you feeling like that, so we can talk about it. Listen, I'm not perfect. But I will never intentionally do anything to hurt you, you have to know that, you have to trust that. That's the only way this works. Ok?" Amara knew Adrian was right, she knew he was nothing like his father and she had to trust that. "You're right, and I do trust you. I just needed to read those articles for myself you know. I just needed to know exactly what he did to those women.

And you are right there is no way you could ever be like him." As they stood in the kitchen, Adrian gathered the newspapers, ready to discard them and leave the past behind. "I think we can get rid of these. They don't need to go with us, unless you want to keep them," he suggested, a sense of closure in his voice. Amara met his gaze with a nod, a weight lifting off her shoulders. "No, we can toss them. I don't need them anymore," she affirmed, feeling a sense of relief wash over her as she let go of the reminders of the past. Just as Amara checked the clock and realized it was already 12:08, she made a quick decision. "I just realized we're out of juice. I'll run to the store and grab some. I'll be back soon," she said, a mix of truth and a need for a moment alone to process the morning's revelations. Adrian reached out to take the opportunity to help. "I can go get it, baby. I'll be back in a flash," he offered, eager to assist. However, Amara gently declined his offer, a smile playing on her lips. "No, it's okay. Every time I send you to the store, you come back with the wrong thing," she teased, planting a quick kiss on his cheek before darting out the door. "Just watch the grits on the stove for me!" she called out as she hurried off, leaving Adrian to tend to the cooking and reflect on the events of the morning. As Amara headed to the grocery store around the corner to pick up some juice, her mind was preoccupied with the events of the morning. She couldn't shake off the feeling of unease that lingered after the discovery of the old newspapers and the revelations about Adrian's father. As she sat in the parking lot, Amara decided to take a moment to check her phone. She went to the truck and got the phone out. She noticed two new text messages from an unknown number. She knew what she would find when she opened the text. Nervously she opened it and found a picture. It was Marcus, she didn't see any blood so she wasn't sure how it was done, but she could tell he was dead from the picture. The second simply read, 'destroy it.' Amara's heart skipped a beat as she realized the implications of the message. What she asked for had been carried out. She needed to destroy any evidence connecting her with what had happened. Startled, she quickly glanced around, a sense of relief washing over her. The threat that Marcus had posed to her life was finally gone. With a deep breath, she tucked the phone away and made her way into the store to grab the juice, her mind still reeling from the unexpected turn of events. She would destroy the phone when she left. Marcus was gone for real this time and now she could finally breathe.

CHAPTER 12

Family Matters

It was the day of her bachelorette party that Sasha had planned for her. They were only 7 days away from the wedding. Amara told Sasha she wanted a chill celebration. She still had a lot to do, and Amara still had a lot on her mind. She was still worried that the events she had set in play would somehow show up on her front door. As the day of the celebration approached, the anticipation in the air was undeniable. Sasha, ever the enthusiastic party planner, had taken it upon herself to organize the event in honor of Amara's upcoming wedding. The celebration was set to be a gathering of friends and family, a joyous occasion to mark the beginning of a new chapter in Amara's life. On the day of the celebration, the venue was adorned with colorful decorations and twinkling lights, creating a festive and welcoming atmosphere. Sasha had spared no detail in ensuring that everything was perfect for Amara, her best friend and soon-to-be bride. As guests began to arrive, the sound of laughter and chatter filled the air, mingling with the soft music playing in the background. Amara was greeted with warm embraces and well-wishes, the love and support of her loved ones surrounding her like a comforting embrace. Sasha beamed with pride as she watched the celebration unfold, her eyes shining with excitement and joy for her dear friend. The party was a reflection of the bond they shared, a testament to the friendship and love that had brought them together. Throughout the evening, guests mingled and shared stories, raising their glasses in toast to the happiness and love that filled the room. The celebration was a beautiful tribute to Amara and Adrian's love, a reminder of the journey they had embarked on together and the bright future that lay ahead. As the night wore on, the music swelled, and the dance floor filled with laughter and joy. Amara found herself surrounded by the people she loved, their smiles and laughter a balm to her soul. In that moment, she felt a sense of gratitude and contentment, knowing that she was surrounded by the love and support of those who mattered most. As the celebration continued, the atmosphere was filled with excitement and laughter as the women gathered for a night of fun and games. Sasha had organized a lively game of "Wedding Trivia" to entertain the guests and test their knowledge of love and marriage. Amara, Evelyn, Sasha, and the other women were seated together, eagerly awaiting the first question. Sasha read out the question, "What is the significance of the 'something blue' in a bride's attire?" The group shared knowing looks and exchanged playful smiles, ready to showcase their wedding trivia knowledge. Evelyn leaned in with a grin and whispered to Amara, "I think it's supposed to represent purity, but I've also heard it's to ward off evil spirits!" Amara chuckled and nodded in agreement, "I've heard that too! It's all about superstitions and traditions, isn't it? Sasha joined in the conversation, adding, "I always thought it was for good luck, but I like the idea of warding off evil spirits better!" Evelyn spoke up and said “before we keep going.” As the "Wedding Trivia" game came to a pause, Evelyn's eyes shimmered with emotion as she reached into her bag and pulled out a small, delicate box. She handed it to Amara, her hands trembling due to her excitement. "Amara, my dear, this is for you," Evelyn said, her voice soft and filled with love. Amara opened the box and gasped at the beauty of the ring before her. “Ma, it’s beautiful. Where di you get it?” Evelyn smiled “This blue pendant ring has been in my family for generations. It belonged to my great, great, great grandmother, a symbol of enduring love and family ties." Evelyn's eyes glistened with tears as she continued, her voice quivering with emotion. "When my grandmother was younger they were slaves. Eventually she and her husband my great, great, great grandfather were freed. One of his goals was to buy his wife this ring. She had saw it in a store, a store people of color wasn’t allowed to enter. He looked and looked for the ring but could never find a store he was allowed to go in that would had anything similar. One day he met this woman, a jewelry maker and he described the ring to her and asked if she could make something similar. The woman told him she wasn’t sure if it would be exactly like it but she could try. She spent 73 days looking for materials and certain colors to make this ring for him. She finally got it finished and he paid 10.00 dollars for that ring. He saved every dime he had to buy it for her, this blue sapphire ring. It was a token of his love and devotion, a promise of a lifetime of happiness together." She paused, her voice catching as she spoke of her own struggles. "I was never blessed with the ability to have children, and I feared I would have no one to pass it on to. But now, seeing you and Adrian together, I know that it has found its rightful place." Evelyn's words were filled with a deep sense of gratitude and love. "Amara, you have brought so much joy and light into my life. I am blessed to have you as a daughter, and I know that this ring will be cherished and loved by you as it has been by generations before us." Amara's eyes welled up with tears as she accepted the gift, her heart overflowing with love and gratitude for Evelyn's gesture. “This is your something blue to wear on your wedding day.” The room was filled with a sense of warmth and connection, the bonds of family and love shining brightly in that moment of shared emotion and love. As Evelyn's heartfelt gift brought tears to everyone's eyes, Sasha was visibly moved by the emotional moment. She reached into her pocket and pulled out a small, intricately designed silver clip lined with real pearls. The clip sparkled in the light, a beautiful and timeless piece that exuded elegance and grace. "Amara, this is something old that I want to pass on to you," Sasha said, her voice soft and filled with emotion. She handed Amara a pretty little box with a bow on it, containing the heirloom pearl clip. "This was my mother's, a beautiful pearl clip that she wore in her hair every day. It was her favorite piece of jewelry, and she always said it brought her luck and happiness." Sasha's eyes glistened with tears as she continued, "On her deathbed, she gave it to me and told me to pass it on to someone I loved, someone who would cherish it as much as she did. I want you to have it, Amara, as your something old." Amara was taken aback by the beauty and significance of the heirloom clip. She carefully opened the box and admired the delicate silver clip adorned with lustrous pearls. The weight of the tradition and history behind it filled her with a sense of reverence and gratitude. Sasha wiped away her tears and explained, "In wedding tradition, the 'something old' symbolizes continuity and the connection between past, present, and future. It represents the bride's roots, her family history, and the enduring love that has been passed down through generations. I know my mother would be happy to see you wearing this clip on your special day." Amara held the pearl clip in her hands, feeling the weight of the tradition and love that it carried. Amara's eyes widened in surprise as she held the pearl clip in her hands, her heart touched by the sentiment behind Sasha's gift. "I never heard that story before, and I've never seen this clip. It's absolutely beautiful," she said, her voice filled with gratitude and wonder. Sasha smiled through her tears, her gaze filled with warmth and affection. "I never shared that story with anyone. It was the one thing I had for myself from my mother, a piece of her that I treasured deeply," she explained. "But I wanted you to have it, Amara. I know my mother would have loved you as her own daughter had she had the chance to meet you." The room was filled with a sense of love and connection, the bond between Sasha and Amara growing stronger with each shared moment. The pearl clip, a symbol of family, love, and enduring legacy, served as a reminder of the ties that bound them together and the love that transcended generations. Amara stood before her friends and family, her eyes glistening with tears of joy and gratitude. "I didn't know I would spend this day crying so much," she began, her voice filled with emotion. She took a deep breath, her heart overflowing with love and appreciation as she turned to Evelyn. "Evelyn, thank you," Amara's voice trembled with emotion, "for loving me like your own, for being the mother I needed when I didn't even know I needed one. Your unwavering support, your kindness, and your guidance have meant more to me than words can express. You've been my rock, my guiding light, and I am forever grateful for your love and presence in my life." As tears streamed down her cheeks, Amara turned to Sasha, her voice filled with a depth of emotion that words could barely capture. "Sasha, my dear friend, my person," she began, her voice quivering with emotion. "I can't imagine my life without you by my side. You have been my confidante, my shoulder to cry on, my partner in laughter and tears." Amara's heart swelled with love and gratitude as she continued, "Thank you for saving me when I felt like I was drowning, for being my light in the darkness, and for always standing by me, no matter what. Your friendship has been a beacon of hope and love in my life, and I am endlessly thankful for your unwavering support and love." Amara turned and faced everyone else, “To all the rest of you, my friends and family. Thank you for always supporting me, thank you for always being there for me. You guys all play such an important part of my life and I truly want to say thank you. Thank you for being exactly who I always needed you to be.” The room was filled with a profound sense of warmth and connection, the love and support of her friends and loved ones surrounding Amara like a comforting embrace. Each word spoken was infused with a depth of emotion that resonated with sincerity and love, a testament to the deep bonds of friendship and family that had shaped her life and filled her heart with gratitude and love. As the bachelor party for Adrian unfolded at the upscale bar where he was a silent investor, an air of exclusivity and sophistication enveloped the gathering. The dimly lit venue exuded an aura of luxury, with plush seating and a well-stocked bar setting the stage for an evening of celebration among men of high stature. The intimate group of guests, carefully curated for the occasion, were seated around a table, savoring drinks and engaging in lively conversation. Laughter filled the air as the men shared stories and engaged in friendly banter, the clinking of glasses adding to the festive ambiance. Just then, the door swung open, and Mayo, a longtime friend of Adrian, strolled in with a confident swagger. Adrian's face lit up as he spotted Mayo, and the two men exchanged a warm smile before dappling each other up in a gesture of camaraderie. "Mayo, my man, good to see you!" Adrian greeted warmly, reaching out to dap him up. "Aye, I need to holla at you later about some business," Adrian added in a hushed tone, hinting at a conversation to come. Mayo nodded in acknowledgment, a knowing look passing between the two friends as they settled in for the evening of celebration and camaraderie. As the evening at the upscale bar continued, the atmosphere was filled with laughter and camaraderie among the men of high stature gathered to celebrate Adrian's bachelor party. The clinking of glasses and the sound of jovial conversation filled the air, creating a warm and welcoming ambiance. Amidst the lively chatter, Harrison rose from his seat, a look of sincerity and warmth in his eyes. "Gentlemen, if I may have your attention," Harrison's voice carried across the room, commanding the room's focus. He cleared his throat, a sense of reverence in his demeanor as he prepared to speak. "I want to take a moment to make a toast to my best friend, Adrian," Harrison began, his voice steady and filled with genuine emotion. "Adrian, my brother from another mother," he continued, his words carrying a depth of friendship and camaraderie. "In the years that we have known each other, you have been a constant source of support, a true friend through thick and thin." Harrison's gaze met Adrian's, a smile of appreciation and admiration on his face. "Your strength, your integrity, and your unwavering loyalty have been a guiding light in my life," Harrison spoke from the heart, his words resonating with sincerity. "I am grateful for the moments of laughter, the shared experiences, and the bond of friendship that we have forged over the years." Raising his glass, Harrison continued, "To Adrian, a man of honor, a man of heart, and a true friend. May your journey ahead be filled with love, joy, and endless happiness. Here's to you, my friend." Everyone toasted and the partied continued. Harrison knew everyone was drinking and soon the entire room would be drunk. He saw Mayo and figured I was the best time to pull him aside and have a conversation with him. Adrian approached Harrison "Hey man, can you grab Mayo and bring him to the back. I figure we can holla at him now before yall fools get too lit out there." Adrian laughed as he walked to the back heading back to a private office. Mayo and Harrison walked in the office behind Adrian. Adrian pulled out a bottle of 1942 from his desk and three crystal glasses. He poured all three of them a drink and instructed both of them to have a seat. "Take a seat man, how you been Mayo? How's the family?" Mayo sipped his drink with a smile on his face, happy to be sitting and chatting with his old friends. "Man everything and everyone is good, you know staying busy and staying out the way. Everything good?" Adrian looked at Harrison and figured this was the best time to bring up their plan. "Actually, there is something we wanted to talk to you about Mayo." Mayo had a look of confusion on his face not sure what Adrian was hinting about. "Ok, was up?" Adrian stood up and sat at the end of his desk. "Mayo, you know we trust you more than anything. You know after Harrison you're the second person I trust more than anybody with my work life. You quiet, you move in the shadows, and I know your loyal. After I get married, the deal I make next week is going to be my last deal. Well, shit it's going to be me and Harrison's last deal." Mayo put his drink down on the table looking at both of them with worry on his face. "Last deal? What you mean last deal, you saying yall out?' Adrian looked at Harrison and smiled. Harrison replied "Yea man, we're out. We been in this game for a long time brother, and it's time we take a few steps back. But of course we can't interrupt business either we have to be sure that keeps going with no interruptions." Adrian looked at Mayo and said "So, we were wondering, better yet thinking, that you could take over operations. The entire empire would be yours." Mayo couldn't believe what they were asking him. He didn't think this would be the conversation they would having tonight. "Hell yea, man. I'll take over this shit you know it." Mayo hopped up dapped up both men and embraced each other. Mayo always knew he would be at the top of the food chain one day, he just didn't think it would be this soon. Adrian poured them all another drink "To good times, and new journeys for all of us." They took their shots and laughed it up. Adrian clapped his hands "let's head back out there fellas, let's finish this celebration right." They all headed back out to the bar with the rest of the guest to finish celebrating. Between turns, jokes were exchanged, and stories shared, adding to the laughter and joy of the evening. The room was alive with the sound of banter and camaraderie, creating a memorable and light-hearted atmosphere for Adrian and his friends.

CHAPTER 13

Dance in the Moonlight

It was Saturday morning of the wedding day, the day dawned with a soft glow, signaling the beginning of a new day and a momentous occasion on the horizon. The wedding day had arrived, bringing with it a sense of joy, love, and the promise of a lifetime of happiness. Amara sat in the serene bride suite, the soft morning light filtering through the sheer curtains, casting a warm glow over the room. The gentle hum of excitement filled the air as the bridal party bustled around her, preparing for the day ahead. The faint scent of fresh flowers and delicate perfume lingered in the air as Amara took a deep breath, savoring the moment. The soft rustle of fabric and the gentle murmur of conversation added to the anticipation and excitement that filled the room. As she settled into the plush chair, the skilled hands of the hair stylist worked their magic, weaving her dark locks into an elegant and intricate updo. Each twist and curl was a work of art, creating a timeless and beautiful hairstyle that complemented her radiant smile. Next, the makeup artist delicately applied each brushstroke, enhancing Amara's natural beauty and accentuating her features. The soft hues and subtle touches highlighted her eyes and lips, adding a touch of glamour and sophistication to her bridal look. As she looked in the mirror, Amara's heart swelled with emotion. The reflection staring back at her was a vision of grace and beauty, a bride filled with love, joy, and the promise of a lifetime of happiness. In that moment, surrounded by the love and support of her closest friends and family, Amara felt a sense of peace and excitement for the day that lay ahead. As Amara's transformation continued in the bride suite, Sasha, her loyal friend and confidante, sat beside her, a look of admiration and joy in her eyes. "Amara, you look absolutely stunning," Sasha whispered, her voice filled with genuine emotion. "You are going to take Adrian's breath away." Amara smiled gratefully at Sasha, her heart warmed by her friend's words. The photographer moved around the room, capturing the intimate moments and the intricate details of the bridal preparations. The soft click of the camera and the gentle guidance of the photographer added to the sense of anticipation and excitement in the room. Amara, nervously stood in front of the mirror in her bridal suite, her hands fidgeting with her veil. The room was filled with the soft hum of excitement as her bridesmaids bustled around her, making final adjustments to her gown. As she heard a gentle knock on the door, her heart fluttered with anticipation. "Come in," she called out, her voice tinged with nervousness. The door creaked open, and Amara's father, David, stepped inside, a small velvet box in his hand. His eyes shone with pride and love as he approached his daughter. "Amara, sweetheart, may I have a moment alone with you?" David asked, his voice filled with warmth. Amara turned to look at her father, a mixture of surprise and curiosity in her eyes. She nodded, setting down her veil and turning to face him. "Of course, Dad. If you guys could give us a few minutes. Come back in about 5 minutes or so.” Everyone cleared out the room and left Amara with her dad alone in the suite. “What's on your mind dad?" Amara inquired, her voice filled with anticipation. David opened the velvet box, revealing a pair of exquisite diamond princess earrings glistening in the soft light of the room. Amara gasped in awe, her eyes widening with delight. "These are for you, my dear. Something new for your wedding day," David said, a smile tugging at the corners of his lips. Amara's hands trembled as she reached for the earrings, her heart overflowing with gratitude and love for her father. She carefully placed the earrings on, feeling their weight and sparkle against her skin. "Thank you, Dad. They're beautiful," Amara whispered, her voice filled with emotion. David beamed with pride as he watched his daughter admire the earrings, a symbol of his love and support for her on this momentous day. He wrapped his arms around her, holding her close in a tender embrace. "May these earrings bring you joy and happiness as you start this new journey, my dear. I love you more than words can express," David said, his voice filled with love. Amara hugged her father tightly, feeling the warmth of his embrace and the love that surrounded her in that moment. As she looked at herself in the mirror, adorned with the sparkling diamond princess earrings, she felt a sense of peace and joy wash over her, knowing that she carried her father's love with her as she walked down the aisle. As Amara stood before the mirror, her eyes shimmering with tears of gratitude and love, she felt a wave of emotion wash over her. The diamond princess earrings sparkled in the soft light, casting a radiant glow around her. She turned to her father, David, who stood beside her with a tender smile on his face, his eyes filled with pride and love. "Thank you, Dad. These earrings are so beautiful. I don't know what to say," Amara whispered, her voice filled with emotion. David reached out and gently brushed away a tear from Amara's cheek, his touch warm and comforting. He took a deep breath, his own eyes glistening with unshed tears as he looked at his daughter, his heart overflowing with love. "Amara, my dear, your mother would have been so proud of the woman you have become. She may not be here with us physically, but her love and spirit are always with you, guiding you on this journey," David said, his voice filled with tenderness.

Amara's heart ached with the memory of her mother, the absence of her presence on this special day palpable. She felt a sense of loss mingled with gratitude for the love and support she received from her father. "I miss her so much, Dad. I wish she could be here to see me today," Amara said, her voice trembling with emotion. David wrapped his arms around his daughter, holding her close in a comforting embrace. He pressed a kiss to the top of her head, his love for her palpable in the silent gesture. "I know, my dear. Your mother is watching over you from above, sending her love and blessings on your wedding day. She would want you to be happy and cherish this moment," David said, his voice filled with love and reassurance. Amara leaned into her father's embrace, feeling the warmth of his love and the strength of their bond. She took a deep breath, finding solace in his words and the precious gift of the diamond princess earrings that symbolized their shared love and connection. "Thank you, Dad. I will carry her love in my heart as I walk down the aisle today. And I will always cherish these earrings as a reminder of your love and support," Amara said, her voice filled with gratitude. David held his daughter close, savoring the moment of quiet intimacy between them. In that moment, father and daughter shared a bond that transcended words, a love that would carry them through all the joys and challenges that lay ahead. As they stood together in the bridal suite, surrounded by love and memories, Amara felt a sense of peace and gratitude wash over her, knowing that she was not alone on this special day. She was surrounded by the love of her father, the memory of her mother, and the promise of a new beginning as she embarked on the journey of marriage. Adrian and Harrison, the groomsmen, stand side by side in their all-white tuxedos, looking sharp and dapper. The room is filled with the rich aroma of cigars, adding a touch of elegance to the air. Adrian takes a long drag from his cigar, exhaling a cloud of smoke as he adjusts his bow tie, a grin playing on his lips. Harrison stands next to him, a mischievous twinkle in his eye as he surveys their reflection in the mirror. "Looking good, Adrian. I must say, the all-white tuxedo really suits you," Harrison remarks, a teasing tone in his voice. Adrian chuckles, running a hand through his hair and flashing a confident smile. "Thanks, Harrison. You don't look too shabby yourself. We clean up pretty well, don't we?" Harrison nods in agreement, a grin spreading across his face. "We sure do. Who would've thought a couple of guys like us could pull off the whole tuxedo look?" As they share a laugh, the tension of the day begins to melt away, replaced by a sense of camaraderie and friendship. Adrian and Harrison have been through thick and thin together, and this moment of levity is a welcome respite before the whirlwind of the wedding ceremony. Taking another puff of his cigar, Adrian turns to Harrison with a more serious expression. "Hey, man, thanks for being here today. Your friendship means the world to me, and having you by my side on this day is everything." Harrison claps Adrian on the shoulder, a genuine smile on his face. "Of course, Adrian. I wouldn't miss it for anything. We've been through a lot together, and I'm honored to stand by you as you take this next step." As they share a moment of quiet reflection, the bond between Adrian and Harrison shines through, a testament to their enduring friendship and support for each other. The all-white tuxedos may be a symbol of elegance and sophistication, but it's the friendship and camaraderie between these two groomsmen that truly shines on this special day. The room is filled with the sound of laughter and the rich aroma of cigars, As the laughter and camaraderie between Adrian and Harrison filled the groom suite, a sudden knock at the door shattered the moment of levity. Adrian's heart skipped a beat as he turned towards the door, a sense of unease creeping over him. Harrison shot him a questioning look, sensing the shift in Adrian's demeanor. Adrian hesitated for a moment before crossing the room to open the door. As he swung it open, his breath caught in his throat at the sight of a woman standing before him, her features etched with years of absence and regret. It was his mother as Adrian and Harrison prepare to accompany their friend on the journey to marriage. As Adrian stood face-to-face with his mother, a whirlwind of emotions churned within him. The sight of her after all these years reignited a storm of anger and hurt that he had long buried beneath the surface. His voice trembled with suppressed emotion as he demanded, "How did you know to come here?" His mother's eyes brimmed with tears as she explained that she had received an invitation in the mail from an unknown sender, with no return address or details. Adrian's frustration boiled over as he struggled to comprehend how someone had orchestrated this unexpected reunion on his wedding day. "Why did you even bother showing up? After all these years of silence, you think you can just waltz back into my life like nothing happened?" Adrian's voice was laced with bitterness and resentment, his hands clenched into fists at his sides. His mother reached out a trembling hand towards him, her voice choked with emotion. "Adrian, please," Adrian moved away from her "Please don't touch me. Why are you here. How are you here?" Adrian's mother walked towards him, "I, I got an invitation in the mail. I assumed it came from you. I assumed you wanted me here." Adrian looked at her "Well you assumed wrong. I don't want you here. I never wanted you here." Adrian looking around trying to figure out how she got there and it dawned on him, the only person who could have sent the invite was his soon to be wife. In no circumstances would Adrian ever yell at Amara, but right now after seeing his mother all he can see is rage, all he could see was red. Adrian stormed down the hallway and made his way to the bridal suite. He stormed into he suite "Everybody out, now. I need a moment alone to speak with Amara." Amara had a look of shock on her face not sure why Adrian was barging in. "Why are you in here, you know it's bad luck to see me before the wedding." Adrian rubs his hand over his head and looks at Amara. "You know what else is bad luck? Seeing the mother who abandoned you show up at your wedding. I'd say that's really bad fucking luck." Amara shocked as she had never seen Adrian upset or even yell at her since she knew him. "Adrian! I never sent your mother anything. I asked you remember, and you said no. So why the hell would I send her an invitation and tell her to come here. I'd never do that Adrian." Adrian looking at Amara his eyes full of tears and anger. He never knew how he would feel seeing her, but seeing her so unexpectedly took his emotions over. "If you didn't bring her here, who did?" Amara stepped towards Adrian and grabbed his hand. "Adrian, look at me," Adrian looked Amara in her eyes. "After today, it's me and you. That's it me and you. I would never do anything to hurt you or anything to hurt us. This is our day, I would never ruin it by brining her here." A tear dropped from Adrian's eye. Amara could see how hurt it made Adrian to see his mother show up today. She wanted to fix this for him right away. "Stay here ok, I'll get rid of her." Adrian looked up "Amara, no you don't have to do that. I can tell her to leave." Adrian didn't continue to put up a fight. Amara left out of the room and went to find Adrian's mother. She walked into the grooms suite, where she found a beautiful woman standing there. "Hi, you must be Tonya, Adrian's mother." Tonya turned around and looked at Amara, "You must be Adrian's fiancé. Wow he did good, you are stunning." Amara looked at Tonya, a smile on her face and stepped towards her. "Yes, my name is Amara, the fiancé. And you are the woman who abandoned her son and never looked back. Why the hell are you here?" Tonya looked at Amara taken back by her comment. She had expected Amara to be more sensitive towards her. Not sure how to respond she said "Listen I got an invitation to be here, I was invited. I thought my son invited me, but it seems he didn't. Someone must be playing a cruel joke or something." Amara was very protective over Adrian and wanted to protect him by all means necessary. "Listen, I don't know how you got an invitation or sent it to you. But by no means were you invited here and you need to leave, and never, ever come back into our lives again. He has family now, he doesn't need you." Tonya looked at Amara still taken back by her approach. "Ok, Fine. I can leave, and I will stay away and stay out of your lives with no problem." Amara stood out of the doorway "Sounds like a perfect plan to me." Tonya walked out the door and left the wedding. Amara walked back to the bride suite where she found Adrian sitting down with his head in her hands. When Amara walked back inside, he lifted his head up. "She's gone baby ok. She's gone. I'm so sorry." Amara said as she started to kiss Adrian around his face. She wanted him to know she was going to always protect him. Adrian grabbed Amara's arm "Hey, hey Amara I need to apologize to you. I'm sorry for how I came at you earlier. I'm sorry for how I yelled at you. Baby that's not me, I swear to you that's never me. I hope I didn't scare you; I would never want to scare you." Amara grabbed Adrian's arm and pulled him up "Stand up and look at me." Adrian stood up and looked at Amara. "You are my best friend, Adrian. You were upset and I understand that. You were caught off guard, and you just responded out of anger. Now, get your ass back down that aisle so I can marry my best friend." They kissed and Adrian left. It was time for them to make the biggest step of their lives together. The wedding scene was a vision of ethereal beauty, bathed in soft white hues that enveloped the space in a sense of timeless elegance. The guests were seated in rows of pristine white chairs, their eyes fixed on the aisle where the bride, Amara, would make her grand entrance. The air was filled with the melodious strains of a saxophone, its soulful notes weaving a tapestry of emotion and anticipation. As the saxophone played her song, Amara emerged at the end of the aisle, a vision of radiant beauty that took everyone's breath away. Her gown, a masterpiece of lace and silk, cascaded around her like a waterfall of white, shimmering in the soft light of the venue. Her veil trailed behind her like a cloud, adding an air of mystery and grace to her ensemble. Adrian stood at the altar, his eyes fixed on Amara as she made her way towards him. His heart swelled with emotion at the sight of her, the love and admiration shining in his eyes like a beacon. He was captivated by her beauty, by the way she moved with grace and poise, her eyes locked with his in a silent promise of forever. As Amara drew closer, the saxophone's melody soared to new heights, underscoring the moment with a sense of magic and wonder. Adrian's breath caught in his throat as he took in every detail of his bride, from the delicate curve of her smile to the sparkle of her eyes that mirrored the love in his own. Their gazes locked in a silent exchange of vows, a promise of love and devotion that transcended words. In that moment, surrounded by the soft glow of white and the sweet melody of the saxophone, Amara and Adrian stood on the threshold of a new beginning, their hearts entwined in a bond that would weather any storm. As Amara reached the end of the aisle and stood before Adrian, the world around them seemed to fade away, leaving only the two of them in a bubble of love and joy. With tears of happiness in their eyes, they exchanged vows that echoed with the promise of a lifetime of love and happiness, sealing their union with a kiss that spoke volumes of their deep and abiding love. As the wedding ceremony continued, the pastor's voice filled the air with a sense of solemnity and reverence. The moment arrived when the pastor posed the question, "Who gives this woman away?" Amara's father, stood tall and proud beside his daughter, his voice steady as he responded, "I do." With a mix of emotions in his heart, he offered his daughter's hand to Adrian, a silent blessing and a gesture of trust in the love that bound them together. The ceremony unfolded with a series of rituals and traditions, each moment steeped in symbolism and meaning. The exchange of rings, the lighting of the unity candle, and the reading of heartfelt poems all served to underscore the depth of love and commitment shared between Amara and

Adrian. As the time came for them to exchange their vows, the air was charged with anticipation and emotion. Adrian took Amara's hands in his, his eyes locked with hers in a silent promise of forever. "Amara, from the moment I met you, I knew you were the one I had been waiting for. You are my rock, my anchor, and my greatest love. I promise to stand by your side through all the joys and sorrows of life, to support you, cherish you, and love you with every fiber of my being. I vow to be your partner in all things, to listen, to understand, and to be there for you in times of need. With this ring, I pledge my heart and my soul to you, now and forever," Adrian's voice rang out with sincerity and love. Amara's eyes shone with tears of joy and love as she took a deep breath, her heart overflowing with emotion. She spoke her vows with a voice filled with love and determination, her words a testament to the depth of her feelings for Adrian. "Adrian, you are my everything, my soulmate, and my best friend. From this day forward, I promise to walk by your side, to support you, and to love you unconditionally. I vow to be your confidante, your partner in adventure, and your source of strength in times of weakness. I promise to laugh with you in times of joy, to comfort you in times of sorrow, and to be a faithful and loving companion for all the days of my life. With this ring, I pledge my heart and my love to you, now and for all eternity," Amara's voice trembled with emotion as she spoke her vows. As the vows were exchanged and the promises of love spoken, the pastor's voice rang out with a sense of solemnity and joy. "You may now kiss the bride," he declared, giving Adrian and Amara the long-awaited moment to seal their union with a kiss. Adrian cupped Amara's face in his hands, his heart brimming with love and happiness as their lips met in a tender and passionate embrace. The guests erupted into cheers and applause, their joy and excitement filling the air with a sense of celebration and unity. "I now present to you Mr. and Mrs. Bishop," the pastor announced, his words carrying the weight of a new beginning and a lifetime of love and togetherness. Amara and Adrian, now officially husband and wife, walked hand in hand down the aisle, their hearts intertwined in a bond that would endure all trials and tribulations. the wedding reception kicked off with an air of celebration and merriment. The venue was transformed into a magical wonderland of twinkling lights, vibrant flowers, and joyful laughter that filled the air. The guests mingled and danced, their spirits lifted by the promise of love and happiness that permeated the atmosphere. Amara and Adrian made their grand entrance into the reception hall, greeted by cheers and applause from their loved ones. The DJ played their favorite song as they took to the dance floor for their first dance as husband and wife, their movements graceful and tender, a reflection of their deep love and connection. The reception program continued with speeches and toasts from family and friends, each one filled with heartfelt words of love and well-wishes for the newlyweds. Ladies and gentlemen, esteemed guests, and of course, the newlyweds - Adrian and Amara! I must say, I never thought I'd see the day when Adrian would trade in his video game controller for a wedding ring! But here we are, celebrating the union of this wonderful couple, and I couldn't be happier to be a part of it. Let me take you back to our childhood, when Adrian and I were partners in crime, causing mischief and mayhem wherever we went. I remember one time we decided to play hide and seek, and Adrian thought it would be a brilliant idea to hide in what he thought was an empty doghouse. Man, this man crawled backwards in the dog house. I'm sitting around looking and looking and I don't find him. It's going on like 10 min, so shot I'm like I give up. I start hearing something like a yell. I'm looking around and then boom I hear it coming from the doghouse. I go over and bend down this fool is stuck in the damn doghouse and can't get out. We had to call the firetrucks to come and get him out of there. So it's like 2 hours go by and they finally get him out. I tell you I wasn't expecting him to say what he said. The firefighter tells him, he sprained his ankle and they were going to put him in the ambulance to check him out. They are loading him on the stretcher, and they are pushing him by me. He stops them and says I have to say something to my brother, please what if I don't make it. He grabs my shirt all dramatic, and says "I still won! Man to this day I still laugh at that story." But on a more serious note, Adrian has always been more than just a friend to me - he's been a brother, a confidant, and someone I can always count on. He's the kind of guy who would give you the shirt off his back, even if it meant he had to wear a leaf as a loincloth. Adrian has always been there for me, through thick and thin, and I am so proud of the man he has become. And then there's Amara - the woman who has captured Adrian's heart and brought out the best in him. From the moment he met her, I could see the change in him, the sparkle in his eye, the spring in his step. Amara, you are truly the woman of his dreams, and I couldn't be happier to see him find his happily ever after with you. So, here's to Adrian and Amara, the dynamic duo, the perfect pair, the video game enthusiast and the love of his life. May your days be filled with laughter, love, and endless joy. And remember, Adrian, if you ever need a break from Amara's cooking, my door is always open! Cheers to the happy couple! Everyone busted out into laughter. It was time for Amara to make her speech next. "Ladies and gentlemen, esteemed guests, and most importantly, the radiant couple - Amara and Adrian. Today, as I stand before you, I am filled with an overwhelming sense of joy and gratitude as I witness the union of two souls who were destined to find each other in this vast and beautiful world. Amara, my person, my best friend, my sister from another mister. From the moment we met as children, our bond was forged through shared laughter, tears, and countless memories that have woven the fabric of our lives together. We have weathered storms, celebrated triumphs, and navigated the complexities of life side by side, hand in hand. We both know the pain of losing our mothers at a young age, the ache of that void that can never truly be filled. But in each other, we found solace, comfort, and unwavering support. Amara, you have been my rock, my confidante, and my guiding light through the darkest of days. Your strength, resilience, and unwavering love have been a beacon of hope in my life, and I am endlessly grateful for your presence in my journey. Today, as I stand by your side as your maid of honor, I am filled with pride and joy to witness the love that you and Adrian share. Adrian, you are the man who complements Amara in every way, who cherishes her, supports her, and loves her unconditionally. Your love for her is evident in every glance, every touch, and every smile, and I am grateful to see her in the arms of someone who treasures her as she deserves. Amara, my person, my best friend, my sister - today, as you embark on this new chapter of your life with Adrian by your side, I want you to know that I will always be here for you, cheering you on, supporting you, and loving you with all my heart. Your happiness means everything to me, and seeing you find the love and joy that you deserve fills my heart with immeasurable happiness. So, here's to Amara and Adrian, the perfect pair, the dynamic duo, the embodiment of love and devotion. May your days be filled with laughter, your nights with love, and your hearts with endless joy. Cheers to the beautiful couple, and to a lifetime of happiness and togetherness. I love you, Amara." As the celebration continued, the time came for one of the most anticipated wedding traditions - the tossing of the bouquet and garter. Amara, beaming with joy and excitement, made her way to the center of the dance floor, her bouquet held high in her hands. The single ladies gathered around her, their eyes alight with anticipation and laughter, eager to catch the coveted bouquet. With a mischievous twinkle in her eye, Amara turned to face her single friends, a playful smile dancing on her lips. With a graceful motion, she tossed the bouquet into the air, the flowers spinning and twirling as they descended towards the outstretched hands of the eager guests. Laughter and cheers filled the air as one lucky lady caught the bouquet, her face lighting up with delight. Not to be outdone, Adrian stepped forward, a sly grin on his face, ready to retrieve the garter from Amara's leg. As he knelt down, his eyes met Amara's, a silent exchange of amusement and love passing between them. With a playful wink, he removed the garter, eliciting laughter and cheers from the guests. Rising to his feet, Adrian held the garter in his hand, a mischievous glint in his eye as he turned to face the single gentlemen gathered nearby. With a flourish, he tossed the garter into the air, the men jostling and reaching to catch it in a lighthearted display of camaraderie and good-natured competition. As the bouquet and garter toss concluded, the dance floor erupted with laughter and joy, the guests reveling in the festive atmosphere of the wedding celebration. Amara and Adrian shared a knowing look, their hearts full of love and happiness as they watched their friends and family come together in a moment of shared merriment and fun. The sound of laughter and music filled the air, mingling with the joy and love that enveloped the room. The bouquet and garter toss had brought a touch of lightheartedness and playfulness to the evening, adding to the sense of celebration and unity that permeated the wedding reception. Amara and Adrian, surrounded by their loved ones, danced the night away, their hearts overflowing with happiness and gratitude for the love and support that surrounded them on this special day. As the wedding celebration drew to a close, the guests gathered outside, each holding a sparkler that cast a warm and magical glow in the night. The air was filled with a sense of anticipation and excitement as Amara and Adrian prepared to make their grand exit and begin their journey as husband and wife. Amara and Adrian emerged from the venue, hand in hand, their hearts full of love and gratitude for the unforgettable day they had shared with their loved ones. The sparklers illuminated their path, creating a shimmering tunnel of light that led them towards their waiting wedding car, adorned with ribbons and flowers. As they walked through the sparkling corridor, Amara and Adrian waved goodbye to their guests, their faces radiant with joy and happiness. The guests cheered and clapped, their voices filled with well-wishes and blessings for the newlyweds as they embarked on their new adventure together. Amidst the twinkling lights and the sounds of laughter and music, Amara and Adrian reached the waiting car, a symbol of the journey that lay ahead. With a final wave to their friends and family, they climbed into the car, their hearts full of love and anticipation for the future that awaited them. As the car pulled away, the sparklers continued to burn brightly, creating a trail of light that followed the newlyweds into the night. Amara and Adrian sat side by side, their hands intertwined, their hearts filled with the love and joy of a day that would forever be etched in their memories. As they drove off into the night, the echoes of laughter and music faded into the distance, leaving behind a sense of peace and contentment. Amara and Adrian looked towards the future with hope and excitement, knowing that they had each other to lean on, to support, and to love through all the days of their lives. And as they journeyed into the night, hand in hand, their hearts were filled with the promise of a lifetime of happiness and togetherness.

CHAPTER 14

What Are Friends For

As the sun's rays gently illuminated the room, Adrian's eyes slowly fluttered open to the sight of his beautiful wife, Amara, lying beside him. A soft smile graced his lips as he reached out to brush a stray strand of hair from her face, his touch gentle and loving. "Rise and shine, Mrs. Bishop," Adrian whispered, his deep voice filled with warmth and affection. Amara rolled over meeting Adrian's gaze. "Well good morning Mr. Bishop." Adrian moved closer to kiss her, "Umm, baby just know I love you so much that I'll smell that morning breath everyday." Amara let out a roar of laughter, "I know you not talking not the way the long ass toenails you got down there cutting me up in the middle of the night. I mean pedicure, get one" Adrian jumped up out the bed and grabbed a pillow "Oh yea," he started a playful pillow fight between both of them. They played around for a few minutes until they both ended up landing on the floor. They laughed and laid there looking at each other. Adrian knew he has somethings he needed to take care of so he needed to leave the house early enough so he wouldn't be too late getting home. "Hey, I need to run some errands this morning and I have a few business meetings with some investors later. I promise it won't be too long, I should be back around dinner time." Amara smiled You better hurry back, Mr. Businessman. I'll miss you, but I'll be here, making sure everything is perfect for our getaway. And who knows, I might just have a surprise or two up my sleeve for you." Adrian chuckled, his heart swelling with love for the woman who never failed to keep him on his toes. "Oh, really now? Well, I can't wait to see what you have in store for me, Mrs. Sneaky. Just remember, I'll be counting down the minutes until I can whisk you away to paradise and show you just how much I adore you." Leaning in, Adrian planted a soft kiss on Amara's forehead, his lips lingering for a moment as he savored the sweetness of their connection. With a final wink and a playful smile, Adrian rose from the floor, his heart light and full of anticipation for the day ahead. As he prepared to head out, he knew that the countdown to their honeymoon had officially begun, and he couldn't wait to embark on this new journey with the woman who held his heart in her hands. As the sun's gentle rays filtered through the windows, casting a warm glow over the room, Amara made her way downstairs to the kitchen to prepare herself some breakfast. The smell of sizzling bacon and eggs filled the air, a comforting aroma that usually brought a smile to her face. As she hummed along to a lively tune playing in the background, she began to dance around the kitchen, her movements fluid and carefree. The music filled the room with its infectious energy, the beat pulsing through her veins as she twirled and swayed to the rhythm. The melody lifted her spirits, the joy of the music enveloping her in a cocoon of lightness and freedom. Lost in the moment, Amara's worries and uncertainties faded into the background as she let herself be carried away by the music. However, as she continued to cook, a wave of nausea suddenly washed over her, causing her to pause mid-dance. The once delightful aroma of breakfast now turned her stomach, and a sense of unease settled in the pit of her stomach. With a gasp, she felt a surge of sickness rising within her, and before she knew it, she was rushing to the restroom, her hand clamped over her mouth as she fought back a wave of nausea. Barely making it to the toilet in time, Amara doubled over, her body heaving as she emptied the contents of her stomach. As she sat there, trying to catch her breath, a whirlwind of thoughts raced through her mind. Could she be pregnant? But she was on the pill, so it couldn't be that, right? Maybe it was just an upset stomach, a passing bout of illness that would soon fade away. Despite her attempts to rationalize the situation, the idea of pregnancy lingered in the back of Amara's mind, a spark of hope and fear intertwined. She took a deep breath, trying to calm her racing heart and quell the rising panic within her. Whatever the cause of her sudden illness, she knew she needed to take care of herself and figure out what was going on. As Adrian settled into the comfortable leather chair in JT's office, the lawyer greeted him warmly, a sense of professionalism and trust emanating from his demeanor. "Good to see you, JT. Thanks for making time for me today," Adrian greeted him with a smile, a sense of familiarity and camaraderie in his tone. JT returned the smile, his eyes crinkling at the corners. "Always a pleasure, Adrian. How have you been? I must say, your wedding was absolutely beautiful. It was a joy to witness your special day," JT remarked, a genuine warmth in his voice. "Thank you, JT. It meant a lot to have you there. It was a day I'll never forget," Adrian replied, a hint of nostalgia in his voice as he recalled the memories of the wedding day. "I'm truly happy for you, Adrian. It's clear to see how much you love Amara, and it warms my heart to see you so happy and in love," JT commented, his words filled with sincerity and genuine happiness for his longtime client. Adrian's smile widened at JT's words, a sense of gratitude and contentment washing over him. "I appreciate that, JT. Amara has brought so much light and love into my life. I want to make sure she's taken care of, no matter what," Adrian shared, his voice filled with love and devotion for his wife. JT nodded in understanding, a sense of respect and admiration in his gaze. "I have no doubt that you'll take care of her, Adrian. Your commitment and dedication to your family are truly commendable. Let's make sure everything is in order to protect your loved ones," JT affirmed, his professionalism and support unwavering. As they delved into the details of Adrian's estate plan, the conversation shifted to discussions about family, love, and the importance of ensuring a secure future for those we hold dear. Adrian shared stories of his journey with Amara, the challenges they had overcome, and the joys they had shared. JT listened attentively, offering guidance and reassurance, his presence a source of comfort and stability for Adrian. As the meeting with JT continued, Adrian shifted in his seat, a thoughtful expression on his face. "JT, I have another request. I need you to set me up with your Private Investigator," Adrian began, his voice tinged with a sense of urgency. JT raised an eyebrow, a curious look in his eyes. "A Private Investigator? May I ask why, Adrian?" he inquired, his tone filled with interest and curiosity. Adrian took a deep breath, a hint of hesitation in his voice. "My mother showed up unexpectedly at the wedding. She mentioned receiving a random invite, but she wouldn't reveal who sent it. I need to find out who it was that gave her that invite. It's been years since I've seen her, and her sudden appearance has left me with more questions than answers," Adrian explained, his words laced with a mix of confusion and concern. JT nodded in understanding, a look of empathy crossing his features. "I see. Family matters can be complicated. I'll make the arrangements with the Private Investigator and ensure they have all the necessary information to look into this for you. As they discussed the details of setting up the investigation, Adrian felt a sense of relief knowing that he had JT's support and expertise in navigating this delicate situation. With the Private Investigator on the case, he hoped to uncover the truth behind his mother's sudden reappearance and the mysterious invitation. As the meeting drew to a close, Adrian extended his hand towards JT, a sense of gratitude and trust evident in his gaze. "Thank you, JT. I appreciate your help with setting up the Private Investigator. I'll be leaving for my honeymoon on Tuesday, so I'll be out of the country for a week. I'll touch base with you when I return, and we can discuss any updates from the investigation," Adrian explained, his voice filled with determination and resolve. JT clasped Adrian's hand in a firm shake, a look of understanding and support in his eyes. "Safe travels on your honeymoon, Adrian. Enjoy your time away, and don't worry about a thing here. I'll make sure the Private Investigator has all the resources they need, and we'll reconvene when you return," JT assured him, his professionalism and commitment unwavering. With a final nod of acknowledgment and a shared understanding of the task at hand, Adrian and JT parted ways, each with a sense of purpose and determination in their respective roles. Adrian left the office with a renewed sense of hope and anticipation for his upcoming honeymoon, knowing that the investigation into his mother's sudden appearance would be in capable hands. As Adrian made his way to the warehouse to meet Harrison, anticipation and a sense of purpose filled his thoughts. He arrived at the warehouse where they conducted their business, greeted by the familiar sight of their operation. Harrison welcomed him with a firm handshake, a knowing look passing between them. "Adrian, good to see you. Shit, you ready to make this last run?" Harrison asked, a hint of excitement and determination in his voice. Adrian nodded, a sense of relief and resolve in his gaze. "Absolutely. It's been a long ass road, but I'm looking forward to moving on to new opportunities. It'll feel good to leave this chapter behind and start fresh. You know not having to look over our shoulders all the time." he replied, his voice filled with a mix of nostalgia and hope for the future. As Adrian and Harrison delved into the specifics of their final deal, the warehouse hummed with the sound of their voices as they discussed the details of their agreement. They outlined the terms, the risks, and the potential rewards, each decision made with precision and care. "Alright, my brother, this deal will give us 15 million. We'll both walk away from this last run with 7.5 million each. With all we have saved over time, all we have invested all we have made. We will be forever good after today." Harrison explained, a sense of satisfaction and pride in his voice. Adrian nodded in agreement, a sense of relief and gratitude washing over him. "Damn right, man the bars been doing good, the properties are doing great, and now we about to own our own apartment building. Shit, man we did what we were supposed to do. The goal was to always get out. I'm just glad we are putting this behind us." As Adrian and Harrison finalized the details of their final deal, Mayo walked into the warehouse, a sense of purpose and determination in his stride. Adrian and Harrison greeted him with nods of acknowledgment, a shared understanding of the importance of this meeting. "Mayo, good to see you. You're joining us for this final deal. We're going to introduce you to the main man we supply, he's who you will be doing business with a lot of the times. You know most of everyone else, but this man here won't do business with you without a proper introduction." Adrian explained, a note of confidence and assurance in his voice. Mayo nodded in understanding, a look of readiness and focus in his eyes. "I'm ready for this, Adrian. I appreciate the opportunity to take over. I appreciate that you trust me to take over everything that you've built. I promise you I won't disappoint yall. I'll keep everything running just as you have always. I'm here to make it count," he replied, his voice filled with determination and resolve. As they prepared to meet with the main man they supplied, the warehouse buzzed with anticipation and energy. As Adrian, Harrison, and Mayo prepared to drive to the meeting spot, they loaded up the car with a sense of purpose and anticipation. The warehouse echoed with the sound of their footsteps as they gathered their belongings and made their way to the vehicle waiting outside.

The engine roared to life as Adrian took the driver's seat, Harrison settled in the passenger seat, and Mayo took his place in the back. The car pulled out of the warehouse, the tires crunching on the gravel as they set off on the journey to the meeting spot, an hour and a half away. The road stretched out before them, the landscape passing by in a blur of colors and shapes. The trio shared a moment of quiet reflection, each lost in their thoughts as they neared their destination. The hum of the engine and the rhythmic sound of the tires on the road filled the silence, a sense of determination and focus settling over them. As Adrian, Harrison, and Mayo pulled up to the warehouse, a sense of anticipation filled the air. The trio exchanged a glance, their eyes scanning the surroundings as they took in their surroundings. Outside the warehouse, a man who appeared homeless was pushing a cart, a sign in his hand that read "spare change." Adrian rolled down the window, reaching into his pocket to retrieve two quarters. The man's eyes lit up with gratitude as he accepted the coins, offering a nod of thanks before moving on. Adrian watched him go, a sense of empathy and compassion in his gaze. Turning to Mayo, Adrian spoke in a low voice, "Anytime you meet him, you will get a text from a random number with the amount of change for the day. Today was two quarters, so I put two quarters in the cup. He will send some sort of signal, and then they will open the gates. If he doesn't give you the clear, you won't get into the gate, and the change has to be exactly how the text says, no exceptions." Mayo nodded in understanding, a look of determination and focus in his eyes. As the man disappeared from sight, the gate to the warehouse opened, signaling their entry. Adrian drove the car inside, the sound of the engine echoing in the empty space. The garage door closed behind them, enveloping them in a shroud of secrecy and anticipation as they prepared to meet with the main man and finalize their deal. Adrian turned to Mayo “Listen when we go in here just stay quiet and listen. We have been suppling this person for years and no one knows. No one in our operation at all. Due to his line of work, we are required to keep it that way, understand?" Mayo nodded his head. "This is going to be one of your biggest buyers and it's like clockwork. You meet him every three months here, make the sale, and it's 2.5 million every three months ok. He will only deal with the direct supplier, never have anyone new come meet him or you'll lose him as a client understand?" Mayo looking at Harrison and Adrian understanding the severity of what he is learning. Harrison chimed in "Don't ask any questions either, about him, his work, nothing. None of that is your business and you don't care. This isn't a regular client he could blow up everything so just follow the rules, get your money, and keep your thoughts to yourself." Mayo a little confused now wondering who it was they were about to meet. A door opens in front of them and a car pulls in. Two men step out from the front and approach the car where Adrian and them waited in. Adrian rolled down the window to verify it was him. Both men nodded which signaled Adrian to open the trunk and rolled the window up. Adrian looked at Mayo "No words, you say nothing. They nod you open the trunk. They will verify what's back there, and signal those in the back. They step out with the money and the make the exchange. You never get out of the car, ok." Mayo nodding curious to who the person was they were making a deal with that required this amount of secrecy. After they made the exchange a man got out the backseat and walked towards the car. He knocked on Adrian's window signaling Adrian to let the window down. "Adrian" Adrian recognized the man at the window and responded "He's in the back" Adrian rolled down the window showing Mayo in the back. The man standing outside of the car looked inside and extended his hand out to Mayo in the back. "I look forward to seeing you in three months." The mysterious man stepped back and walked off. He got in the car and as the doors closed the truck pulled off. Mayo still had a look of confusion on his face. “Aye, am I tripping but I feel like I saw that man before. Isn’t he the right hand to,” Harrison turned around told Mayo to stop talking right away. “Listen, another rule, don’t mention any names, nothing. You don’t recognize anybody you see ok. Never speak on it. Got it?” Mayo understood, he nodded his head and said “Ok. I got it” Alright. As Adrian, Harrison, and Mayo headed back to the warehouse to unload everything, the car was filled with a sense of accomplishment and relief. Mayo turned to Adrian and Harrison, a curious look in his eyes. "So now that y'all are out, what's the plan?" Mayo asked, his voice filled with curiosity and anticipation. Adrian smiled, his gaze softening as he thought about the future. "Well, the plan is to start a family with Amara. I want to focus on building a life together, creating a home, and maybe having some little ones running around. It's time to shift gears and embrace a new chapter," he shared, his voice filled with warmth and excitement at the thought of starting a family. Harrison nodded in agreement, a sense of contentment and peace in his expression. "For me, it's about enjoying life and focusing on the condos we'll be building. I want to take some time to relax, travel, and savor the moments of freedom. It's about living in the present and appreciating the journey," he explained, his voice tinged with a sense of tranquility and joy at the prospect of a new beginning. As Adrian, Harrison, and Mayo arrived back at the warehouse, a sense of accomplishment and relief washed over them. Adrian handed Mayo a bag containing $500,000 as a token of appreciation for his assistance that day, a gesture of gratitude for his part in the successful deal. "Here, Mayo. This is for you. You've been a valuable part of the team today, and we appreciate your hard work," Adrian said, his voice filled with sincerity and appreciation. Mayo accepted the bag with a grateful smile, a look of surprise and gratitude in his eyes. As Mayo prepared to take over the enterprise for Adrian and Harrison, Adrian handed him the keys to the warehouse, a symbol of trust and confidence in Mayo's capabilities. "Take care, Mayo. You're ready for this next step, and we have full faith in your leadership. Keep in touch, and let us know how things go. The future is bright with you at the helm," Adrian said, his voice filled with pride and assurance. Mayo nodded, a sense of determination and readiness in his gaze. "Thank you, Adrian. I will continue the legacy you've built and lead with integrity. I appreciate this opportunity and look forward to the journey ahead. Take care, and I'll be sure to keep you updated," he replied, his voice filled with gratitude and commitment to the new role. As Mayo stepped into his new position, Adrian and Harrison stood in the warehouse, a sense of closure and new beginnings settling over them. They looked around at the space that had been the heart of their operations, memories of their journey flooding their minds. "This marks the start of a new era for us, Harrison. Mayo is ready to lead, and it's time for us to embrace the next chapter," Adrian remarked, his voice filled with a mix of nostalgia and excitement for the future. Harrison nodded in agreement, a sense of pride and satisfaction in his expression. As Mayo headed out, Adrian and Harrison stood in the warehouse, a sense of nostalgia and reflection settling over them. They looked around at the space that had been the center of their operations for so long, memories of their journey flooding their minds. "This is the end of a major era for us, Harrison. We've come a long way, and now it's time to start a new life and a new journey," Adrian remarked, his voice filled with a mix of affection and excitement for the future. Harrison nodded in agreement, a sense of pride and satisfaction in his expression. "It's been quite a ride, Adrian. But I'm ready for what's next. Shit, life is good man. And now we can live it in our truth and safely." he replied, his voice filled with determination and hope for the future. As they looked ahead to the new beginning that awaited them, Adrian and Harrison knew that they were ready to embrace the challenges and adventures that lay ahead. With a shared sense of purpose and unity, they were prepared to embark on a new chapter of their lives, ready to build a future filled with promise, growth, and success. Adrian and Harrison got in the car both of them their suitcase full of 7.5 million. They were ready to take on their new journeys. The warehouse door opened, and they began to pull out. As the fence opened Harrison pulled out in his car and went to the left. Adrian was pulling out and went to the right. He was driving through the red light when out of nowhere a car came flying and crashed into the drivers side of the car. Adrian's truck went flying and flipped four times. Harrison was half a mile down the street but saw the crash. He went to turn around and that's when he saw the driver of the car in all black and masked up. He jumped out the car and grabbed the suitcase of money out of the back seat. Harrison was racing down the street, by the time he made it the man had gotten in his car and drove off. He went to check on Adrian, he didn't have a pulse. Harrison was screaming for someone to call the police and the ambulance. Harrison was holding his best friend in his arms, blood was everywhere. "Adrian, you can't do this to me man. You can't die on me man. Come on you got to make it. You got to live, you got Amara. You just started a new life, come on man, please don't die on me. Don't die Adrian." Within minutes you could hear the sirens approaching. The paramedics got there, Harrison got up out of the way, "Please he just got married, please save him." Harrison knew he had to call Amara; he didn't want to. He pulled out his phone and dialed her number. "Harrison, hey, don't tell me my wonderful husband's phone is dead again." Harrison was silent at first, he wasn't sure what to say. "Amara, it's Adrian. I'm so sorry." As Harrison left, Amara's mind raced with a mix of emotions and thoughts. She knew she needed to act swiftly and decisively in the wake of the startling revelation about Adrian's past. With a sense of urgency, Amara reached for her phone and dialed Sasha's number, her fingers tapping anxiously as she waited for her friend to pick up. "Sasha, it's Amara. I need you to come over right away. It's urgent, and I need to talk to you in person. Hey Sash watch your back." Amara said, her voice filled with a sense of urgency and determination. Sasha on the other line confused, but responded "Ok, I'm on the way Amara." As she spoke to Sasha, Amara began packing a few essentials, her movements swift and purposeful. She knew that time was of the essence, and she needed to act quickly to ensure her safety and protect herself from the unknown dangers that Adrian's past had brought into her life. She couldn't leave without talking to Sasha first, but she needed to speak to Sasha before she left. As she awaited Sasha's arrival, Amara's mind raced with a mix of fear and determination. As the doorbell rang, Sasha let herself in, a sense of urgency and concern in her expression as she found Amara sitting in the kitchen, a drink in her hand, and her bag packed. The weight of the recent events hung heavy in the air, casting a somber shadow over the room. Sasha rushed to Amara's side, her eyes filled with worry and compassion as she enveloped her best friend in a tight hug. Tears welled up in both their eyes as the weight of the recent tragedy washed over them, the raw pain and grief of losing Adrian palpable in the air. Amara clung to Sasha, her shoulders shaking with silent sobs as she found solace in the comforting embrace of her friend. Sasha held her close, offering a silent presence of support and understanding in the face of unimaginable loss. "I'm so sorry, Amara. I can't imagine what you're going through. I'm here for you, whatever you need," Sasha whispered, her voice filled with empathy and sorrow as she held her friend close. Amara's voice trembled with emotion as she spoke, her words choked with tears and heartache. "It's all so overwhelming, Sasha. I never imagined... I never thought... How do I even begin to process this? How do I move forward from here?" she uttered, her voice breaking with the weight of her grief. Sasha listened, her heart aching for her friend as she offered a comforting presence in the midst of the storm. "You don't have to have all the answers right now, Amara. It's okay to grieve, to feel lost, to be angry. Just know that you're not alone. I'm here for you, every step of the way," Sasha reassured her, her words a beacon of support in the darkness of despair. As the weight of the recent revelations settled over them, Amara took a deep breath, steeling herself to share the unsettling truth that Harrison had revealed about Adrian's past. The room was filled with a heavy silence as she gathered her thoughts, her hands trembling with a mix of fear and determination. "Sasha, there's something I need to tell you. Harrison... Harrison told me about Adrian. He wasn't who I thought he was. He was... he was involved in something dangerous, something criminal. I don't know all the details, but I'm scared, Sasha. I'm scared for my safety, for your safety. I need to get out of town before someone comes looking for me," Amara explained, her voice filled with a sense of urgency and fear. Sasha's eyes widened in shock and confusion, a mix of concern and disbelief crossing her features. She had never seen Amara so shaken up, so upset, and the gravity of the situation weighed heavily on her. "Dangerous what do you mean? Dangerous" Amara looked at Sasha "He was some kind of drug lord or something, I don't know. Harrison just said that he lived a dangerous life and that him and his people are going to find out who did this to Adrian, and some kind of war is coming." Amara started to cry again, "Sasha, I don't know what's happening. I just got married, and now my husbands dead. He was a drug dealer, he was someone completely different then I thought he was. I, just I just don't know what to do Sasha." Sasha looked at her friend, "Amara, breath ok. In and out, please just breath." Amara looked at Sasha and followed her as she breathed in and out. "Amara, I... I don't know what to say. I had no idea. I've never seen you like this before. We need to get you out of town, we need to keep you safe. I'll do whatever it takes to help you, to protect you," Sasha replied, her voice filled with determination and a fierce loyalty to her friend. As the reality of the danger that lurked in the shadows sank in, Amara and Sasha knew that they had to act quickly to ensure Amara's safety and well-being. As Amara and Sasha finished packing up the essentials that Amara could take with her, a sense of urgency and determination filled the room. The weight of the situation hung heavy in the air, casting a somber shadow over their preparations. Each item carefully placed in the bag held a memory, a reminder of the life they were leaving behind. As they looked around the room, the familiarity of their surroundings took on a bittersweet hue, each object a piece of the life Amara was leaving behind. Sasha's eyes met Amara's, a silent understanding passing between them as they prepared for the journey ahead. Amara's car pulled up in front of the house. "Thank you, Sasha. For everything. I couldn't do this without you," Amara said, her voice filled with gratitude and emotion. Sasha's eyes glistened with unshed tears, a mix of sadness and determination in her gaze as she embraced her friend. "Amara, you don't have to thank me. I'll always be here for you, no matter what. We'll get through this together," Sasha replied, her voice filled with a fierce loyalty and unwavering support for her friend. "My car is here; I have to go Sasha. Don't worry about me, ok. I'll reach out to you when I know I'm safe," Amara said, her voice tinged with a mix of determination and reassurance. Sasha nodded, a silent agreement passing between them as they prepared to part ways. "Amara, please be careful. I'll be waiting to hear from you. Stay safe, and remember, I'm always here for you," Sasha replied, her voice filled with emotion and sincerity. Amara hugged Sasha, she loved her best friend she had been there for her through everything. "I'll call you when I can. I love you Sash." Amara got into her uber and the car drove off. Sasha waved goodbye, as she watched her friend drive off heading to a destination she didn't know. She was worried but knew her friend was doing what was necessary to save her own life.

CHAPTER 15

Going Ghost

Four years had passed since Amara left everything behind her. She found herself living in the serene beauty of Jamaica, a place that had become her sanctuary and her refuge. The lush landscapes, the warm embrace of the sun, and the soothing rhythm of the ocean waves had offered her a sense of peace and healing that she had longed for. Thinking on the past two years she remembered how she got to the place she was now. Amara made her way to the bank, a sense of urgency and determination filled her heart. The weight of the recent revelations about Adrian's past lingered in her mind, casting a shadow of uncertainty over her thoughts. With each step she took, she knew that she was stepping into a new chapter of her life, one defined by courage and resilience. Upon reaching the bank, Amara approached the safety deposit box that had remained unopened for years. With trembling hands, she unlocked the box and found within it a passport with her picture but a different name, a substantial sum of money, and a letter from Adrian.

'Hey baby, if you're reading this letter that means, I'm gone, and you now know the truth of who I really am. I am so sorry for lying to

you, and not being honest with you. I want you to know I love you. I promised to protect you no matter what and that's exactly what I'm going to do. In this box you'll find a passport with a new name, a cell phone for you to use that can't be traced, money to get you through for now, and a number. You need to assume a new identity. If you are here right now that means you don't know who killed me so that leaves you at danger until they find out. 404-555-6555 Contact Jason Thompson, my lawyer after you get to where you're going and set up your new identity. He knows this name and if I'm dead he'll be expecting your call. He will set you up for the rest of your life. You will never have another worry again. Amara please be safe and take care of yourself. Burn this letter after you get it don't trash it, you don't know who's following you. Be safe, I love you. Adrian."

As she reflected on the events of that day, the echoes of Adrian's words in the letter resonated within her, a mix of love, regret, and longing that tugged at her heart. The weight of his final message, filled with sorrow and remorse, lingered like a haunting melody, a reminder of the complexities of their shared past .In the quiet of her thoughts, surrounded by the memories of the past and the uncertainties of the future, she was interrupted by a small quiet but dainty voice "mommy," Amara smiled at the sound of her daughters voice, "Well hello, my sweet baby. How are you?" Amara's voice was filled with tenderness and affection as she lifted her daughter into her arms, her eyes sparkling with love and adoration. Her daughter, a spitting image of her late husband, gazed up at her with eyes that mirrored his, a mix of innocence and curiosity shining within them. As Amara twirled her daughter around in the air, a sense of joy and contentment washed over her, the weight of the past momentarily lifted by the lightness of her daughter's presence. The room filled with the sound of their laughter, a melody of love and happiness that echoed through the space. In that moment, surrounded by the memories of the past and the uncertainties of the future, Amara found solace in the simple joy of being a mother, of nurturing and cherishing the precious life that had been entrusted to her care. As she held her daughter close, the complexities of their shared past faded into the background, replaced by the pure and unconditional love that bound them together. In the embrace of her daughter's laughter and the warmth of her presence. As Amara and her daughter strolled along the sun-kissed beach in Jamaica, the beauty of the island enveloped them in a sense of peace and tranquility. The crystal-clear waters lapped gently at the shore, the palm trees swayed in the tropical breeze, and the golden sun cast a warm glow over the landscape. Amara's daughter skipped ahead, her laughter ringing out like music in the air. Amara watched her with a smile, her heart filled with gratitude for the life they had built together. The bond between mother and daughter was unbreakable, a source of strength and joy that carried them through each day. Their footsteps led them back to the stunning beachfront home that Amara had built, a sanctuary nestled amidst the lush greenery and overlooking the azure waters of the Caribbean Sea. The house was a masterpiece of modern design and island charm, with open-air living spaces, expansive windows that framed breathtaking views, and a soothing color palette inspired by the natural beauty of the surroundings. The spacious living room was bathed in sunlight, with comfortable furnishings that invited relaxation and serenity. The kitchen, a chef's dream, boasted sleek countertops, state-of-the-art appliances, and a large island where Amara loved to prepare meals for her family. The bedrooms were havens of comfort and luxury, each thoughtfully designed to offer a peaceful retreat at the end of the day. The master suite, with its plush king-sized bed and private balcony overlooking the ocean, was a place of solace and rejuvenation for Amara. As she prepared breakfast in the sunlit kitchen, the aroma of freshly brewed coffee and sizzling bacon filled the air. The sound of the phone ringing interrupted the peaceful morning, and Amara wiped her hands on a towel as she answered the call. "Hello?" Amara's voice was filled with warmth and curiosity as she greeted the caller. The voice on the other end was familiar, a mix of concern and familiarity that brought a smile to her face. It was Sasha, her dear friend, reaching out from afar to check in and connect across the miles. "Hey Sasha, how's everything going? I miss you so much." Sasha replied "Hey sis, how are you and my God baby doing over there?" Amara replied with a huge smile on her face, "She is good honey, sitting here ready to stuff her face of course. How is everything your way." There was a pause, a moment of hesitation before Sasha continued, her tone somber and heavy with emotion. "Amara this isn't a social call. I have some news. Amara, I don't know how to say this, but your father... he passed away." Amara's heart skipped a beat as the weight of Sasha's words sank in. The news hit her like a wave, a rush of emotions flooding her thoughts. The loss of her father, the man who had been a pillar of strength and support throughout her life, was a blow that left her reeling. Tears welled up in Amara's eyes as she struggled to process the news. Memories of her father, his laughter, his wisdom, and his unwavering love for her, flooded her mind. The ache of his absence pierced her heart, a deep sense of loss settling over her like a heavy shroud. Amara finally found the ability to respond, "Passed away, what do you mean? He's dead? What happened?" Sasha took a breath and said "He had a heart attack Amara. His heart was bad. He was diagnosed with heart failure last year, but he didn't want to tell you. He knew you would try and come back to see him, but he was worried because you know we still don't know who killed Adrian. Apparently, he didn't want you risking your safety or Sarai's safety trying to come and see him." Amara's voice trembled with emotion as she tried to find the words. "I'm catching the first flight back to Atlanta. I have to come check on my family. I need to see Evelyn. Sasha, I, he's gone? You're sure.

My dad is dead?" There was a moment of silence for a few seconds, before Sasha said "Yes, Amara he's gone." Amara closed her eyes, trying to recall the last memory she had with her father, which was him walking her down the aisle. She hadn't seen him since her wedding day, when she left she didn't want to endanger anyone in her family so she felt it was best to stay away at least until they found Adrian's killer. Now with the news she had just gotten she had to go back to Atlanta. She didn't care who might be after her there was no way she wouldn't go back home to bury her father. "Sasha, I'll call you and let you know my flight details ok, can you pick us up?" Sasha, who hadn't physically seen her best friend in over 4 years was happy to meet Amara at the airport and pick them both up. "Of course just let me know what time and I'll be there." Amara ended the call with Sasha. As Amara and Sasha ended their emotional call, a heavy silence settled over Amara as she made her way to the kitchen. The weight of the news about her father's passing lingered in the air, a mix of sorrow and memories flooding her thoughts. Amara poured herself a drink, the clink of ice cubes against the glass a stark contrast to the quiet of the room. As she sipped the drink, memories of her father flooded her mind. His laughter, his wisdom, his unwavering love for her - all woven into the tapestry of her life. Feeling a surge of emotions, Amara retrieved her wedding book from a shelf, flipping through the pages filled with memories of her late husband and now, her late father. Tears welled up in her eyes as she traced her fingers over the images, the bittersweet nostalgia of the past washing over her like a wave. As she sat lost in her thoughts, her daughter Sarai walked into the kitchen, her young face filled with concern. "Mommy, why are you crying?" Sarai's voice was soft and filled with innocence, a reminder of the purity and simplicity of childhood. Amara wiped away her tears, offering her daughter a sad smile. "Oh, sweetheart, I'm just feeling a little sad" As Sarai looked at the photo album in her mother's hand, a sense of innocence and curiosity shone in her eyes. "There's Grandpa, Mommy," she remarked, pointing to the photo that brought tears to Amara's eyes. The memories of her father flooded her heart, a mix of sorrow and love intertwining in her thoughts. Amara's tears continued to stream down her face, but a glimmer of inspiration sparked within her. "Yes, baby, that's Grandpa. Hey, how about we take a trip? Want to go see Aunt Sasha and Granny Evelyn?" she suggested, her voice filled with a mix of excitement and hope. Sarai's eyes lit up with joy and anticipation. "Yes, I want to see them," she exclaimed, her enthusiasm contagious as she took off running to her room. "I'm going to pack, Mommy," Sarai called out, her footsteps echoing down the hallway. Amara watched her daughter's retreating figure, a sense of gratitude and love filling her heart. As Amara watched her daughter, Sarai, excitedly pack for their upcoming trip to Atlanta, a sense of purpose and determination filled her heart. She made her way to her room, the weight of her decision to return to her roots guiding her steps. The memories of her father and the longing to be with her family pulled her towards the next chapter of her journey. In the quiet of her room, Amara began to pack her bag, the familiar routine bringing a sense of focus and clarity to her thoughts. She booked a flight to Atlanta that left the next day at 8 am. As she finalized her preparations, Amara picked up her phone and sent a text to Sasha. The message read, "Flight lands at 11 am. Can you pick me up then?" The simple words carried a sense of connection and anticipation, a reminder of the friendship and support that awaited her on the other side. With her bags packed and her plans in place, Amara stepped out onto the balcony of her bedroom, the soothing sound of the ocean waves washing over her like a familiar lullaby. As she gazed out at the horizon, the memories of her family, her father, and the love that bound them together flooded her thoughts. The ache of loss mingled with the hope of reunion, a bittersweet mix of emotions that tugged at her heartstrings. As Amara's plane touched down in Atlanta, a mix of anticipation and nervous excitement filled her heart. The familiar sights and sounds of the city welcomed her back, the memories of her past and the promise of reunion with her loved ones guiding her steps. Stepping out of the airport, Amara's eyes scanned the crowd until they landed on Sasha, who was waiting for her with open arms. The moment their eyes met, a wave of emotion washed over them, the years apart melting away in an instant. "Amara, it's so good to see you," Sasha's voice was filled with warmth and happiness as she held her friend close. Amara's eyes sparkled with joy as she replied, "Sasha, it's been too long. Thank you for being here." Sarai, Amara's daughter, stood by her side, her eyes wide with wonder as she took in the sight of her godmother for the first time in person. Sasha knelt down, her face lighting up with a smile as she greeted Sarai, "Hey Tt baby, It's so wonderful to finally meet you in person. You've grown so much!" Sarai's face broke into a wide grin, her excitement bubbling over as she replied, "Hi, Aunt Sasha! I'm so happy to see you!" Sarai jumped in Sasha's arms embracing her with a huge hug. The air was filled with laughter and chatter as the three of them made their way through the parking lot, the promise of togetherness and connection weaving between them like an invisible thread. The reunion was a celebration of love and friendship, a reminder that no matter the distance or time apart, the bonds of family and friendship remained unbreakable. As Amara settled into the car with Sasha and Sarai, a sense of anticipation and emotion filled the air. The hum of the engine and the rhythm of the road provided a backdrop for the reunion that awaited them at her father's house. Amara turned to Sasha, her voice tinged with a mix of excitement and nostalgia. "Sasha, do you mind taking me by my father's house first? I want to see my family and pay my respects," Amara's words carried a sense of longing and reverence, her heart heavy with the memories of her father and the need to be with her loved ones in this moment. Sasha nodded, her eyes filled with understanding and support. "Of course, I know your family will be glad to see you," she replied, her voice filled with compassion and empathy for her friend's emotions. As they drove through the familiar streets of Atlanta, Amara and Sasha shared stories and memories of the past, the laughter and chatter filling the car with a sense of warmth and connection. Sarai listened intently, her eyes wide with wonder as she soaked in the tales of friendship and family that wove between her mother and godmother. The car pulled up in front of the familiar home, the sight of it bringing a flood of memories and emotions to the surface. Amara took a deep breath, her hand reaching out to grasp Sasha's for support. She hadn't seen her family in four years, and her father was gone. She didn't know how to feel, she just wanted to see her step mom more than anything. As Amara stepped through the threshold of her father's house, a mix of emotions washed over her. The familiar sights and sounds of the home she had grown up in greeted her, the memories of her childhood flooding back with each step she took. The air was filled with a sense of anticipation and nostalgia as she made her way further into the house. The sound of footsteps approached, and Amara's stepmother, Evelyn, appeared in the doorway. Her eyes widened in joy as she caught sight of Amara standing before her. The shock and surprise mingled with a deep sense of longing and love as she took in the sight of the daughter she hadn't seen in so long. "Amara, my baby girl, is that really you?" Evelyn's voice trembled with emotion as she rushed forward, her arms outstretched in a gesture of love and longing. Tears welled up in her eyes as she brought Amara in a tight embrace, the years apart melting away in an instant. Amara's heart swelled with a mix of emotions as she felt her stepmother's embrace, the warmth and familiarity of the gesture bringing a sense of comfort and solace. As Amara stood in the embrace of her stepmother, Evelyn, a torrent of emotions surged through her. The weight of the past and the realization of her absence during her father's illness weighed heavily on her heart. Tears streamed down her face, a mix of sorrow, regret, and longing intertwining in her thoughts. "I didn't know, Evelyn. I didn't know he was sick. I wasn't there for him when he needed me the most," Amara's voice quivered with emotion as she spoke, the ache of guilt and sorrow piercing her heart. The memories of her father, his strength, his love, and his unwavering care for her flooded her mind, each moment a painful reminder of her absence during his time of need. Evelyn held her close, her own tears mingling with Amara's as she whispered words of comfort and understanding. The shared grief and the weight of their loss bound them together in a moment of raw emotion and shared sorrow. The realization of her father's illness, his struggles, and the burden he had carried alone tore at Amara's soul. The longing to turn back time, to be by his side, to offer comfort and care in his hour of need, was a heavy burden that she carried with her. In the quiet of the embrace, surrounded by the echoes of the past and the weight of her regrets, Amara found solace in the love and understanding that Evelyn offered. As Amara and Evelyn walked into the kitchen, the warmth of family and familiarity enveloped them. The air was filled with the comforting scent of home-cooked meals and the sound of laughter and chatter as everyone gathered around the table. Sarai's presence brought a sense of joy and curiosity to the room, her bright eyes taking in the new faces and surroundings with wonder. Amara turned to Sasha, a sense of determination in her gaze. "Sasha, would you mind taking me somewhere? There's something I need to do," she asked, her voice filled with a mix of purpose and anticipation. The weight of her request lingered in the air, a sense of urgency guiding her steps. Sasha nodded, her eyes filled with understanding and support. "Of course, Amara. I'll take you wherever you need to go," she replied, her voice a beacon of reassurance and friendship in the midst of uncertainty. Turning to Evelyn, Amara's gaze softened as she spoke, "Evelyn, would you mind watching Sarai for a little while?

I need to take care of something, and I want to make sure she's in good hands." Her words carried a sense of trust and gratitude, a reminder of the bond between mother and daughter, and the strength of family ties that bound them together. Evelyn smiled warmly, her voice filled with love and understanding. "Of course, Amara. Sarai will be in good hands. Go take care of what you need to do, we'll be here waiting for you," she reassured, her words a testament to the unwavering support and love that surrounded them. As Amara and Sasha got into the car, the engine revved to life, the familiar hum of the vehicle providing a backdrop to their journey. Sasha turned to Amara, a look of curiosity in her eyes. "Ok, where you want to go?" she inquired, her voice filled with a mix of anticipation and readiness to support her friend. Amara took a deep breath, her gaze fixed on the road ahead. "I want to go back to my house," she replied, her voice tinged with a mix of nostalgia and determination. The memories of their life together, the love and laughter that had filled the walls of their home, beckoned her back to a place that held a piece of her heart. As they neared the house, Sasha guided the car down the familiar streets, the sight of the home they had shared with Adrian coming into view. Amara's heart swelled with a mix of emotions. She had never sold or rented out their house, a decision born out of a deep sense of connection and love for the home she and Adrian were supposed to build together. Sasha parked the car, and Amara stepped out onto the familiar sidewalk, the weight of the past and the promise of closure guiding her steps. As she approached the front door, a mix of emotions washed over her - the ache of loss, the longing for what once was, and the hope for healing and acceptance. As Amara stepped into the house she had once shared with Adrian, a wave of memories washed over her. The familiar scent of the home, a mix of lavender and cedarwood, filled the air, wrapping her in a cocoon of nostalgia and longing. Unpacked boxes still sat on the floor. The furniture, the decor, all remained untouched, frozen in time like a snapshot of their life together. Amara had arranged for a cleaning service to come in once every three months, but she had always instructed them not to move anything. The house retained the essence of their shared history, a time capsule of love and loss that beckoned her to walk its familiar halls once more. Amara moved through the rooms, her footsteps echoing in the silence of the house. The living room, where they had shared countless movie nights and lazy Sunday mornings, the kitchen, where they had cooked meals together and danced to music playing in the background, each space held a piece of their story, a chapter in the book of their life together. She paused in the bedroom, the bed still neatly made, the sunlight filtering through the curtains casting a warm glow over the room. The memories of their late-night conversations, the whispered promises, and the shared dreams lingered in the air, a bittersweet reminder of the love they had once shared. Amara walked over to the cabinet, her fingers tracing the familiar outline of a bottle of wine. She uncorked it with a soft pop, the scent of red grapes filling the air. Pouring herself a glass, she took a sip, the rich flavor dancing on her tongue like an old friend. She turned on some music, the soft melodies filling the room with a sense of warmth and nostalgia. As she settled onto the couch, the memories of her life with Adrian flooded her thoughts. The laughter, the tears, the quiet moments shared in the embrace of their home - each memory a thread in the tapestry of their love. The music played on, a backdrop to the symphony of memories that enveloped her. She closed her eyes, letting the familiar tunes wash over her like a gentle wave. The rhythm of the music matched the beat of her heart, each note a reminder of the love and joy that had filled their home. As Amara sat on the couch, lost in the melodies of the music and the memories of her life with Adrian, a faint ringing caught her attention. The sound was unfamiliar, a jarring interruption in the quiet of the room. She glanced around, searching for the source of the sound, her heart beating a little faster with each passing moment. Though she didn't recognize the ringtone, she instinctively reached for her own phone, checking the screen for any notifications. Finding nothing, she furrowed her brow in confusion, the mystery of the ringing phone adding to the sense of unease that had settled over her. Her gaze fell on the box in front of her, rumbling and vibrating as she kept hearing the phone ring. Amara looked around a sense of nervousness had came upon her. As she opened the box, her hands trembling slightly, she found a phone nestled on top of some old papers. With a deep breath, Amara answered the phone, a mix of shock, concern, and confusion swirling within her. "Hello?" she spoke tentatively, the sound of her own voice echoing in the silence of the room. "In the shadows of the night, the truth shall be revealed. The masks will fall, and the light will shine on the darkness within." The words hung in the air, a chilling reminder of the mysteries that lay ahead. Before Amara could respond, the voice continued, "Midnight Serenade, 12 am, room 4788." The message was delivered with a sense of urgency and finality, leaving Amara with a sense of unease and curiosity. As Amara's mind raced with thoughts and fears, a chilling realization crept into her thoughts. Could it be Marcus, her ex, the man she had set up to be killed years ago? Marcus sent those similar messages to her when he was stalking her last time. Everything, the sense of foreboding and mystery, all pointed to Marcus. Amara had tried to kill him, of course he would be angry. Her mind went back to the day she had orchestrated his downfall. She remembered sending Marcus a text telling him she had the money and to meet her at the hill at 12pm. She knew she had sent someone there to wait for Marcus, and to her understanding Marcus died that day. But what if he had never been actually dead? What if he had been hiding this entire time, waiting for the perfect moment to exact his revenge? The thought of Marcus coming for her, his anger and resentment simmering beneath the surface, filled Amara with a sense of fear and helplessness. As the fear and determination surged within Amara, she knew she couldn't afford to ignore the looming threat of Marcus. If it was indeed him behind the message, she had to face him head-on and put an end to the danger he posed. Marcus was a threat to everything she had built and worked for, and she couldn't let him unravel all that she had put in place. Amara made her way to her old bedroom, the memories of her life with Adrian mingling with the urgency of the present. She entered the closet, her hands shaking slightly as she opened the safe hidden within. Amara retrieved her gun, a weapon she had kept for moments of dire need. The weight of the gun in her hands brought a mix of emotions - fear, resolve, and a sense of protection. She knew that if it was Marcus, she had to be prepared to defend herself and those she loved. As she held the weapon in her hands, a sense of determination settled over her. The memories of her past, the shadows of her mistakes and regrets, mingled with the urgency of the present. Amara knew that she had to confront Marcus, to face the threat head-on and put an end to the danger that loomed over her like a dark cloud. As Amara left the house, she felt a mix of determination and fear. She got back into the car with Sasha, who was waiting for her. The car started, and they drove off, heading towards Amara's father's house. Amara asked Sasha to drop her off there, as she needed to stay with her stepmother, Evelyn, for the night. As Sasha pulled up to Amara's father's house, she turned to her friend with a concerned look. "Amara, are you alright? You seem a bit shaken," Sasha asked, her voice filled with care and worry. Amara forced a smile, trying to downplay her emotions. "Oh, I'm fine, Sasha. Just a lot on my mind, you know how it is," she replied, her voice steady but her eyes betraying a hint of unease. Sasha studied her friend for a moment, sensing that there was more to the story. "If you ever need to talk about anything, I'm here for you, Amara. You don't have to go through this alone," she reassured, her words a beacon of support and understanding. Amara nodded, touched by Sasha's words of support. "I know, Sasha. Thank you for always being there for me, I'll text you in the morning, ok." she said, her voice filled with gratitude. She leaned in and gave her friend a hug, the warmth of their friendship a source of comfort in the midst of uncertainty. With a final smile, Amara exited the car and made her way into her father's house. She walked in quietly it was about 11pm she didn't want to wake anyone. She went to check on Sarai, she was sleeping peacefully in Amara's old bedroom. She went in and kissed her on her forehead. Amara walked out of the room closing the door behind her. She went down to the kitchen and poured herself a drink. She didn't know what to do. The voice on the other end of the phone told her to be at the Midnight Serenade at 12. It was 11:09 she was 34 minutes from the hotel. She had contemplated back and forth if she was going to go to the hotel. She hadn't made up her mind. She thought about what would happen if she didn't show up and Marcus went to the police. Marcus knew too much and she tried to hire someone to kill him. He could ruin her life, and then she'd lose Sarai. She decided she had to do what was necessary to protect her daughter. She had already lost her father, there was now way she could lose her mother too. She pulled out her phone and called an uber to take her to the hotel. She left a note for Evelyn, 'Went out to clear my head. I love you' Amara's uber arrived, and she went outside to get in. She had her gun in her purse, she kept going over and over in her head what she was going to do when she got there. She played it out in her head, how will shot him and no one hear it. She would have to try and claim self-defense. So she thought of ways to provoke him, make him hit her so if she shot him, it wouldn't seem suspicious. She had come up in her head a plan that she figured would work. Marcus had a record he had been put in jail for violence before, and he had a CDV charge, it would be easy for her to shoot him and claim self-defense. She has a gun license so her carrying her gun wouldn't be out of the ordinary. She had made the decision, tonight she was going to kill Marcus, and get rid of him for good. The uber finally pulled up to the hotel, and Amara got out. She looked at the outside of the hotel, the tall beautiful building. She was getting nervous not sure if going up to the room was a good idea. She took a deep breath and entered in the front of the hotel. She made her way to the elevator where she went up to the fourth floor. She saw the sign for 4700-5000 to the right. She finally approached room 4788. Amara stood on the outside, still unsure of what to expect, or exactly who to expect on the other end of the door. Amara went her purse looking around she pulled out her gun, took it off safety and cocked it back. She wanted to be prepared just in case. As she walked towards the door she could see the door was cracked up. Whoever was inside as expecting her. The lights seemed to be out, Amara couldn't see any lights coming through the crack at all. She walked closer and pushed the door open slightly. She opened it enough for her to walk through. Nervous she slowly entered the room, her gun in her hand. As she walked in she called his name "Marcus, I know it's you. I've got a gun so don't try nothing stupid." A lamp on the table, flicks on and illuminates the room. Amara can see someone standing in the shadows, she points her gun, yelling out "I will shoot, come out so I can see your face," The shadow moves closer to Amara and then she finally sees their face. Amara shocked, drops the gun, she looks at the person who emerged from the shadows of the room, with heavy emotion in her voice and tears in her eyes Amara recognizes their face, "Adrian, oh my God, what, no, no, but you're, I thought," Adrian walked towards Amara extending his hand to her. Amara walked backwards not knowing what to believe not sure if the person before her was real. Amara shook her head "Get away from me, Adrian is dead. He died in a car, car accident." Adrian trying to calm Amara down, "Amara baby it's me, it's me Adrian." Amara ran into a corner fear in her eyes and got into fetal position, she wasn't sure what to believe she thought her mind was playing tricks on her and she was going crazy. She covered her ears and started rocking, shaking her head saying no, no, no over and over again. Adrian kneeled down there with her and started to tell her a story that only the two of them would know. "We went to the park one day, we were running 3 miles, you had tried this new water you saw on tiktok. You ordered it and it was your first time drinking it. It was supposed to give you crazy energy. We were running and then out of nowhere you had to pee." Amara looked up at Adrian in his eyes recognizing the story he was telling her. "You went to pee in the bushes trying to hide so no one could see you. You didn't realize that you peed in poison ivy. You got a rash on your butt for like two weeks," Adrian let out a little giggle. Amara now realizing that Adrian was in front of her, she was in complete and total shock. For the past four years she thought this man was dead, and here he was standing before her alive and well. Amara had a different reaction to Adrian being alive then he thought she would. She didn't jump into his arms or leap to kiss him. She was more concerned, more curious as to how he was there and why was he there. Amara stood up and backed a few feet from Adrian, and asked "How?" Adrian sat down at the table, the day after our wedding, me and Harrison went to make a final deal. I was getting out the game. I met you an I wanted everything to be legit. I didn't want anyone or anything jeopardizing our future together. So, I set everything in motion to get out. I went to the warehouse to make a final deal with one of my major clients everything seemed to have went good. Then the next thing I knew a car came out of no where and hit me. After that I don't really remember much, when I woke up I was in DEA custody. They told me I had a heart attack on the scene so I guess when buddy checked me I was dead. But by the time the paramedics got there they were able to restart my hear. Apparently, the DEA had been watching me and had enough evidence on me to send me away for very long time. They had been building a case against me and Harrison, but they wanted someone who was even bigger than us. The had reason to believe that I had been supplying drugs to a federal judge and they wanted to bring him down. They started talking to me about the runs I made up to Savannah Georgia. They told me they had proof and if I didn't help them they would throw Harrison and you into prison." Amara stopped him "But I didn't know anything about his. You told me you sold real-estate." Adrian stood up walking towards Amara again, "I know and I'm so sorry for lying. But the DEA wouldn't have cared that you didn't know, you could have went down just from being with me, they could have assumed you knew and made a case against you. I just couldn't take that chance. But if you turn witness to the Feds, with the amount of information I had, I had to go into witness protection. Nobody could know I was still alive. So they faked my death, allowed you to reap my death benefits, and recreated an entire new identity for me. Amara still shocked, still in disbelief. On top of all of that I still didn't know who tried to have me killed "So, you mean to tell me, this entire time you've been alive. Living carefree, while I sit around missing you, going through hell everyday! Only being able to remember you through memory. Never being able to hold you, to touch you to kiss, you!" Adrian grabbed Amara, "No, don't touch me, don't ever touch me. You were supposed to be dead, gone! I already grieved you, we already grieved you!" Amara screamed. Adrian paused when he heard we, "What do you mean 'We' who is we?" Amara looked at Adrian with regret in her eyes, and sadness. "Our daughter, Sarai, we already grieved you. She already accepted that daddy is her angel that watches over here, and now what do I tell her, umm that daddy's a lying piece of shit." Adrian sat back in his chair trying to process what he had just heard, "Daughter? Amara are you telling me we have a daughter." Amara sat down in the chair beside Adrian, "Yes, we have a daughter." Amara pulled out her cell phone and pulled up some pictures of Sarai. "Her name is Trinity Sarai. She's 3 years old and she's so full of life. Amara showed Adrian a video of Sarai running around on the beach, her counting and saying her numbers, she should him videos of how silly she was. Adrian became overwhelmed with emotion and he started to cry. He had no idea Amara was ever pregnant. "Amara why didn't you tell me you were pregnant? Why did you keep this from me?" Amara responded, "I didn't know until after I left. I went to Jamaica since we already had the tickets for our honeymoon. I got over there and I just stayed. It was peaceful there, and then about 6 weeks later I passed out and I was taken to the hospital. They checked me and told me I was pregnant. So I stayed in Jamaica. They still hadn't found out who tried to kill you so I didn't know if it was safe to come back or not. So, I stayed there. We started to build our lives there, and then I got the call that brought me back here. Adrian confused about what Amara meant, "What call?" Amara looked at Adrian, "It's my father, he um, he passed away. His funeral is a few days and then me and the little one are heading back." Adrian felt remorse for Amara right away, "Amara I'm so sorry to hear that, I had no idea. Are you ok, do you need anything?" Amara hopped up out of her chair still in shock, "I need to know why now, if you didn't know my dad was dead how did you know I'd be here, how did you know I'd be at the house." Adrian leaned back and told Amara the other part of his deal, "Well, I there was another part of my deal. I requested a surveillance camera be put outside the front of the house it's motioned detected, anytime anyone pulls in front of the house the motion detector goes off and it notifies me. I had a cell phone put in there the day they relocated me just in case you ever showed up. I didn't know if you would sale the house or rent it out, but I always hopped you didn't and you didn't. Then tonight I saw on the camera, and I had you meet me here." Amara still confused, "But the voice on the phone belonged to a woman." Adrian told her it was a voice changing software. Amara still confused and not sure how to feel walked over and sat on the bed. "I still can't believe you're alive, you're still here." Adrian walked over to bed and sat next to her. "Yes I'm still here, and I'm so sorry for the pain I caused you Amara, I'm sorry for the hurt I caused you, I'm sorry for all of it. If I had known about Sarai there is no way I would left. Please forgive me, I beg of you please." Amara looked at Adrian, she couldn't sit here and not pretend she wasn't happy to see her husband. They stared at each other, and there was a magnetic pull between them that seemed so strong. As their faces got closer something hit Adrian, "Hold, Amara, when you walked in with the gun in your hand, you said Marcus. Why did you think it was Marcus who left a message for you, on a phone, in our house?" Amara taken back by the question wasn't sure what to say. She knew she could try and lie to Adrian, but it would sound like bullshit. She had just found her dead husband was alive, there was no reason to continue hiding her secrets. She told Adrian everything. She told him about the messages Marcus started sending her, she told him about them getting married in the first year they knew each other. She told Adrian the real reason behind their marriage. Marcus had forced her to help him rob a couple they had met. Amara use to d it with him all the time, she would entertain the couple at a dinner party and then Marcus and his friends would leave and rob them blind. Well one couple caught on to them, and ended up finding out it was them. The prosecution was calling me to testify. Amara told Adrian that Marcus told her the only way to protect both of them was to get married so she couldn't testify against him. So that's what they did they got married. She also told Adrian that she was super rich after her mother died. Her mother left her 2.5 million dollars that she got when she was 21 years old. Marcus also told her that she could never divorce him because he would take her to court for half of everything. "So, I stayed married to him, and then eventually he started black mailing me. I had started making a name for myself in the photography business, I had a brand. But Marcus knew things about me that could ruin my brand and everything I worked so hard for. So he started making me pay him 5000 a month, and I did. Until he started leaving me those messages. I went to meet him and he told me he needed 25,000 and he would be increasing the monthly payments to 10,000 a month. Adrian was visibly upset with every word he was hearing. "Amara why didn't you come to me? Why didn't you tell me?" Amara shook her head, "I didn't want you to know I was still legally married to him, nor did I want you to know about some of the things I had did in my past. So, instead I called this guy that I'd known from back in the day. He was known to get rid of problems, and didn't cost that much. So I hired him, to get rid of my problem." Amara started biting her lip, "So when I got that call and that message on the other line, I thought it was him. I thought somehow he survived and it was him coming at me again. So I cam in prepared to finish the job myself this time. That's why I said Marcus." Adrian couldn't believe what he was hearing. He never imagined that Amara was capable of anything like that, he always assumed she was so soft in everything she did. Adrian stood up looked at Amara and walked up to her, "Listen, we both have past that neither of us were proud of. We did shit that we hid from each other because we wanted to protect the other person. I don't know what you want to call it but I'm going to call it love. Amara, I want to leave with you and Sarai. I want to come to Jamaica, we have more than enough money they won't find me. Amara had a look in her eyes, "What do we tell Sarai that you just came back from the dead?" Adrian pulled Amara into his embrace, "I don't care what we tell her we can figure that out later, all I know is I don't want to spend another second without you or her in my life. Daddy's coming home." Adrian picked Amara up and wrapped her legs around his waist as he carried her to bed and laid her down. As he started to undress her she didn't want Evelyn to awake and be worried about her. "Hold on I don't want Evelyn worried, let me send her text." Adrian looked at Amara, "Amara, you can't tell anyone I'm alive not right now." Amara knew she had to keep this all to herself. She sent Evelyn a text that said "I'm staying at the old house tonight, I just need to try and find some closure. I love you ma, give Sarai a huge kiss for me. I love you both." Amara put the phone down and turned back to Adrian. They started at each other again, and Amara fell into Adrian's arms. He kissed her entire body and slowly undressed her. It had been four years since they had made love and he missed the touch of her. Adrian and Amara made love all night long into the sun rise came through the window. Amara woke up next to Adrian a man she had once planned to spend the rest of her life with. Then all of a sudden he was taken away from her just for him to now be back. She didn't know how to feel. She turned over and looked at the clock it was 8am. She needed to leave her and Evelyn had to be at the funeral home at 10am. She needed to get back so she could shower and get herself dressed. She woke Adrian up with a kiss, he rolled over and saw her laying next to him. He kissed her on the forehead, "I thought I'd never get to do this again." Amara smiled, looking at Adrian, "Yea, tell me about it" she kissed Adrian, as she got up and got her clothes. I have to get back to my dad's me and Evelyn have to be at the funeral home at 10. Amara went into the rest room to freshen herself up. She came out dressed in a rush. "Hey you, I'm going to be back tonight ok. The funeral is tomorrow, we'll flight out right after, and we can start over fresh. No lies between us. It will be just our family. We can figure the rest out later ok." Amara kissed Adrian passionately as she turned to leave out the door. "My uber is outside." Before Amara walked out the door she turned to Adrian, "I love you Adrian." Amara walked out of the hotel room and waited for the elevator. Her mind was still spinning at what happened. She never expected for Adrian to be alive, and to be in that hotel room. She was confused and knew she couldn't tell anyone about him still being alive, she had to keep it to herself. The elevator finally came and she got on. Inside the hotel room Adrian made sure all the blinds were pulled he wasn't planning to the leave the hotel, leaving would put him at the chance of being seen. He was walking and stepped on something small, he looked down and saw it was a small cell phone. He had never seen it before and knew it wasn't his. He was sure he saw Amara leave with her cell phone in her hand so he wasn't sure what it was. He picked up the phone, it was a burner phone. There was no lock code. He checked the contacts and the only number in the phone was an unknown number. There was no missed calls, just some text messages, 'he's not dead, you screwed up' then there was a response 'no refunds' another text which was a picture. "It was a man in all black with a ski mask on. You couldn't see anything but his eyes. The picture was far back but you could still see the eyes. Under the picture there was a text that said 'Either you fix it, or I rat us both out.' Adrian stared at the picture he felt that the eyes of the man felt so familiar. He zoomed in on the picture and he had a memory flash-back. Adrian saw himself laying on the ground in his truck he had just crashed. A man got out of the drivers seat and stood over him in all black and a ski mask. Adrian couldn't remember exactly what he saw he was fading in and out, but then he saw the eye there was a scar on his eye. He looked back at the photo Amara had sent to this random number, it was the same scar the man who tried to kill him had. Adrian's brain started to become overwhelmed. He wasn't con-necting the dots, why would Amara be texting the man who tried, to...and that's when it hit him. He had it wrong the entire time, he couldn't figure out who was trying to kill him because nobody from his street life was trying to kill him. It was Amara. Amara tried to have him killed. Adrian ran to the window trying to see if he could see her walking out he spotted her walking out the front of the hotel towards her uber. He needed to stop her, but before he could move, a black car pulled around the corner, shots started to ring in the air, Adrian watched every bullet hit Amara. Each bullet that hit her knocking her back until she hit the ground. Adrian screamed "Amara!" Adrian threw on his clothes an ran down out of his room down the stairs to Amara. Adrian ran out of the hotel, and downstairs to Amara's side. He grabbed her while she was bleeding out on the concrete, "Amara please don't die. Please I need you to stay with me Amara. I don't care what you did, I don't care why did it, please don't leave me Amara. Please stay with me. What will tell our daughter? You can't die." Amara looked up at Adrian, she lifted her hand and touched Adrina's face, with her last breath she said "I had too, he took everything from me." With those final words Amara took one last breath and died in Adrian's arms. Adrian cried out as he held his dead wife in his arms. He didn't know what to do. The ambulance and police came and processed the scene. Adrian gave his statement told them what he saw from his window. He couldn't tell them everything. Adrian went back up to his room after meeting with them it was after 12 he knew her family was worried about her by now, or they had probably seen the news. Adrian knew he had to come out of hiding he had to go to her fathers. He got dressed, and he called a uber to come and pick him up. He took an uber to Evelyn's father house. He got out the car and he could see all of the cars everywhere. He had a hat on trying to conceal his identify the best he could until he walked into the house. Adrian knocked on the door, and he saw a little girl run to the door, he recognized her from the videos Amara showed him. Sarai looked at Adrian with a confused look on her face. She recognized him but only as an the angle that watches over her. "Daddy?" Adrian opened the door and leaned down to be face to face with Sarai. "Hi Sarai, how are you?" Sarai smiled big and threw her arms around Adrian's neck "Daddy, daddy,!" Adrian squeezed Sarai hard as tears streamed down his face. Adrian heard Evelyn, calling for Sarai from inside the house, "Sarai who is that at the door, is that your moth..." Evelyn met Adrian's face as she walked to the door, she dropped her rag and let out a scream, "Oh my God!" Everyone in the house ran to the front door to make sure Evelyn was ok. They all saw Adrian holding Sarai, and it stopped them in their tracks. Sasha, came from around the corner her eyes full of shock and surprise. Not sure what was going on. "Give me her, give me my God daughter." Adrian didn't put up a fight she knew they were in shock seeing him because they all thought he was dead. Evelyn still in shock looked at Adrian, "Who are you?" Adrian walked towards Evelyn, "Ma, it's me." Evelyn shook her head, "No, no. My son in law died in a car crash. We buried him, no, no. Where is my daughter? Where is Amara what is going on?" Adrian looked at Evelyn and Sasha, with remorse and sadness in his eyes. His eyes welling with tears. Sasha holding Sarai, walked towards Adrian, "You heard her, where the hell is Amara?" Adrian looked at Sasha and shook his head, "Amara, Amara's dead."

www.ingramcontent.com/pod-product-compliance
Ingram Content Group UK Ltd.
Pitfield, Milton Keynes, MK11 3LW, UK
UKHW021700190726
13853UKWH00001B/381